SPY IN THE TUNNEL

For Special Agent Waltham, assigned to the village of Hamilton in Vermont, the problem was difficult from the start. Among the townspeople was someone who was acting as intermediary for couriers arriving from Canada with money and instructions for the Apparatus people in the United States. When Peter Waltham finally discovered who the person was, life became difficult because a million and a half dollars disappeared. By the time he was on the right trail, peril was closing in on all sides.

Other books by John Morgan
in the Linford Mystery Library:

MURDERERS DON'T SMILE
THE MIDNIGHT MURDER

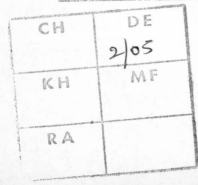

JOHN MORGAN

SPY IN THE TUNNEL

Complete and Unabridged

LINFORD
Leicester

First published in Great Britain in 1969 by
Robert Hale Limited
London

First Linford Edition
published 2005
by arrangement with
Robert Hale Limited
London

British Library CIP Data

Morgan, John, *1916 –*
Spy in the tunnel.—Large print ed.—
Linford mystery library
1. Detective and mystery stories
2. Large type books
I. Title
823.5′4 [F]

ISBN 1–84395–576–8

Published by
F. A. Thorpe (Publishing)
Anstey, Leicestershire

Set by Words & Graphics Ltd.
Anstey, Leicestershire
Printed and bound in Great Britain by
T. J. International Ltd., Padstow, Cornwall

This book is printed on acid-free paper

1

Hampton House

It was called Hampton and at the base of the southernmost wing there was a carefully inscribed number: 1690.

Once, the Methodist Lady's Community Aid Association undertook to exhume Hampton's past. There had, thirty or forty years earlier, been a journal, kept during the War of the Rebellion by one Brigadier Jeremiah Hampton, but it had disappeared a few years later, no one knew whether by accident or design, and this of course worked a great hardship on the Methodist Ladies.

Another thing that troubled them was the way owners came and went after the Rebellion. For example there were letters in the Vermont Historical Society addressed to a Gordon, a Jedediah Julian, and one George Windsor, all evidently former tenants or owners of Hampton, or at least they got their mail there, yet neither the Historical Society nor the Hall of Records where deeds and mortgages had been recorded since the initial settlement of the New Hampshire Grants, had any records of those three gentlemen at all.

Moreover, since there were other Good Works for the Methodist Ladies — petunias to be planted round the bases of trees in the local park at Hamilton, meetings of the Hamilton Literary League, and physical support of the Hamilton Ministerial Association — the Hampton undertaking was gradually pushed farther and farther down the agenda of Things To Be Done.

Some wag even suggested that the number 1690 did not refer to the year of erection, but meant instead there were 1,690 fieldstones between base and baulk. It didn't take long to prove that incorrect. Then someone else, caught up in the spirit of the thing, suggested 1,690 fieldstones from that inscribed cornerstone round the house at the base and back to the cornerstone again. No one bothered to make the count this time, for in Hamilton in the year 1969, the Hampton estate was scarcely relevant; it was no longer necessary to build New England manor houses of stone with walls three feet thick, adequate for defence against skulking Six-Nation redskins, or the equally as skulking, but not so successful at it because of their scarlet coats, British Regulars down out of Montreal to punish a covey of homespun colonials. And too, with the fading need for such a formidable residence as Hampton House, sitting as it did upon its low hill, trees and underbrush burnt out in all directions, cannonshot-distance, the actual *dis*advantages were promptly apparent.

For example, since Vermont winters were long, cold, and clammy-damp, old Hampton House was a veritable tomb, inside. Additionally, plumbing, for which the place had not been originally engineered, and which had subsequently been installed about the time of the War Between The States, for reasons of prestige more than anything else, had never functioned properly. And despite valiant efforts of several tenants since the installation of electricity, once, during World War One, rats dining on insulation had shorted the wiring and caused the roof to burn, while another time a lightning strike had so over-loaded the circuits in all directions the place had popped and sparked like a fireworks display, the then-owner, an Israel Putnam, had suffered a minor heart seizure and had moved out three days later, after which Hampton House lay vacant for three years, then the father of the present owner, Kingsley Lee, had bought it.

Old Mr Lee, known locally but not to his face as 'King' or 'Old King' had spent a fortune on the great grey stone pile. All wiring had been encased in aluminium conduit, all iron plumbing pipe had been replaced with copper, and a huge diesel-fuel heating system, with forced-draught ducts through the attic to each room, had been installed in the great, dungeon-like cellar.

Kingsley Lee, confidant of Presidents and Board Chairman of Eastern & Ottawa Railroad, had been a very influential, wealthy, and pompous man. He died shortly after the return of his only son, Frank Lee, from service in the Second World War. In fact, he was the second permanent guest of the family plot he'd established in the quiet and hoary Hamilton cemetery, the first being his wife who pre-deceased him by some eleven years.

Thus it had been Kingsley who had finally modernised old Hampton House. No one prior to his era, evidently, had possessed either the motivation, or the money. In fact, after the pyrotechnics which had caused old Putnam's small heart attack it had been suggested at a Town Council meeting in Hamilton that the old castle-like edifice be torn down, the rocks sold and the land subdivided. Only a suggestion; no one had the kind of money it would have taken to undertake so ambitious a project. Demolishing Hampton House which had originally been built with deflection of British cannonballs in mind, would involve a lot more knowledge and expertise than the merchants of the Hamilton Town council possessed, or were prepared to hire. And in any case, shortly afterwards along came 'Old King' Lee to relieve them of this burden.

There was, in one of the glass cases at the Historical Society's musuem, a frail, faded old free-hand drawing of the floorplan of Hampton House. It had an illegible signature and no date, but was generally thought to be either the original architect's concept, or perhaps the working plan for the initial builder — whoever he was, although one could not help but still admire, after practically three hundred years, his genius as a stone mason.

This plan still applied; there was no way to alter the floor-plan, but over the centuries dozens of owners had altered the arrangement of rooms time and time again. Presently, Frank Lee and his wife, Emily, lived exclusively on the ground floor, but previous owners had all had their bedrooms and sitting-rooms upstairs. Further, the first floor had been richly panelled so none of the stone still showed. Their son, Walter, after his first year at college, had moved his bedroom back upstairs, which made him the only resident of the second floor although there were seven more bedrooms and five nice sitting-rooms up there.

The servants, a man and wife named Carl and Dorothy Bronson, had their own apartment off the rear pantry, complete with a converted buttery used for television viewing.

It cost a small fortune to heat Hampton House, especially since the summers in Vermont were little more than a three months interlude of intruding sunshine. But the Lees had the money, old Kingsley had seen to that. And both Frank and his wife loved the estate. They had never found the pair of vaults shown on the old plan in the museum, and now, in their middle years, no longer amused themselves by trying, although they frequently let houseguests search to their heart's content. Frank had said rather often, that after growing up in Hampton House, and being by nature a curious and prying child, if the original builder had not obviously balked at the additional expense of making those places, he'd certainly have found them because the old map was very specific.

He was right, of course, and to prove it, once he and Walter, plus two college friends of his son's down for a holiday weekend, had actually torn out a part of a wall to show that regardless of the old floor-plan, there was no vault at all.

It had cost a thousand dollars to bring in a qualified stonemason to heal that scar and Emily hadn't thought any of it was very funny.

The other vault, allegedly behind the fireplace with access, so far as the old plan showed, through the rear wall of fire-brick, had only half-heartedly been searched for because of a very basic reason: Nine months out of the year there was a fire on that hearth, and those three remaining months there had quite often been a fire to take the chill off the great parlour in the evenings.

As Frank told Walter; 'It doesn't make

much sense. How could anything be secreted behind the fireplace anyway? If someone *did* manage to open the wall somehow, then managed to crawl through a fire, or over hot coals, and get the damned wall closed after himself, if the smoke didn't strangle him back there, the infernal heat would.'

Walter, a Korea War veteran completing his medical internship at Massachusetts General down in Boston, average height like his father, blue-eyed and stocky, showed the same smile as he nodded and turned to consider the huge old fireplace. As his mother came to announce that Dorothy had dinner on the table, Walter said, 'You're probably right,' to his father, and added, 'With winter coming maybe we'd better not duplicate the demolition undertaking again.'

Emily needed no explanation. She was a handsome woman, sturdy like her husband and son, but dark-eyed and dark-haired where they were both fair. She drew herself up.

'Frank, I've heard you say a dozen

times there are no hidden passages at Hampton. But you still tore out that wall, didn't you?'

Frank smiled tenderly and used his most soothing tone of voice. He'd gone over the border to French Canada to marry, and over thirty years later he would still attest there were no more beautiful, generous, lively and devoted wives on earth than French-Canadians. But they were also volatile and liable to be so practical at times it was appalling.

'We were just talking, Em,' he said. 'There was no mention of tearing out the fireplace's back-wall.'

'Yes,' retorted Emily, hands clasped across a flat stomach. 'You just talked about the wall too.' The hands sprang away and gestured. 'It is the end of summer, Frank. But even if that were not so, how in the world would you ever put it all back again? Ah! If the wall cost a thousand to repair, what would that huge fireplace cost?. Now come to dinner. Walter, have you washed?'

Walter was not just a medical intern, he was also a veteran of a war and a man of thirty, not a lad of ten. Still, he laughed as he said, 'I'll wash at once,' and left the room.

Emily swung dark eyes from the empty doorway back to her husband. 'If you tear out that fireplace, Frank, I will spend a month in Quebec with my sisters and brothers until you have cleaned up the mess. I swear, you are incorrigible.' Emily rolled her eyes, made a slight gesture of supplication, then turned towards the baronial dining-hall.

Frank had a cold pipe in his hand which he placed upon the shelf at his back, and stood for a moment longer gazing beyond the silent-burning logs on the ancient stone hearth to the fire-brick wall in back.

Then he shrugged and went trooping after Emily to the dining-room. It was August, still hot during the day but beginning to have a faint hint of chill after dark, and he'd been walking a good deal lately, so he was hungry. There was, also, the matter of cholesterol, for, rugged as he was, Emily was a worrier. After Walter moved to Boston she'd turned all her protectiveness towards Frank. He didn't object; in fact, he rather liked being pampered again. There had been a long period in between when it hadn't happened.

2

Special Agent Peter Waltham

'There are two things I can tell you,' said Special Agent Waltham to his chief in Washington. 'One: this place up here — Hamilton — is the drop, and two, their local lad is one of the established people.'

The voice on the long-distance connection said, 'Why does their person have to be a local, Peter?'

'Chief, this is New England. Small-town New England. These people just naturally read the return-address on envelopes, manage to study the registration slip of your car, and when you send a suit out to be cleaned, they first look at the labels. There's no chance of a stranger coming here just to arrange the meetings. I've talked to two dozen people since landing here. Not one of them said there had been any strangers stay more than a week.'

'Are there any strangers in Hamilton right now, Pete?'

'No sir. Hamilton isn't an exactly unique New England town because it has no river or lake close by, but this time of year, in the daytime at least, people seem to be more concerned with keeping cool than with seeing quaintness. The last visitor drove off several weeks ago.'

'All right, I'm convinced. Now tell me which of the locals might be our man?'

'Chief, I haven't the foggiest idea.'

'All right. Another question, Pete: How do they make their transfers?'

Waltham sounded exasperated as he said, 'I don't know that either. I'll admit I've been here a week and it's a small town, but unless I want to rouse a lot of suspicion, which the other side would detect, I've simply got to stay here, go on playing the holidaymaker until another courier arrives, then take it from there.'

'Keep me informed, Pete. Goodbye.'

Waltham settled the telephone back upon its cradle, went to the open window of his second-floor room at the Hamilton Hotel, considered the street below, with the bank, drug store and haberdashery across the way, and leaned to scan the countryside beyond. Out there stood that old manor house people called Hampton. It stood upon a low, rolling hill with broad acres of grassland all around. In one way Waltham thought it looked terribly romantic; like some old English manor house. In another way he thought it would make an ideal setting for ghost stories.

He left the window, went to put away the suit that had been returned from the cleaners a bit ago, and beneath it was the manila folder he'd taken from its hiding place to re-read just before telephoning down to Washington. After putting the suit in a closet he returned to the folder. It had no label, and inside, although there were what appeared to be cryptographic numerals and letters atop each page; there were no headings, no signatures, and even when it referred to some specific individual, it always did so by some variation of the word 'principal.'

There were forty-four double-spaced

pages to this report and Pete Waltham had read, and re-read, them all. In summary it was very simple. Communist couriers in the United States had been traced back to the village of Hamilton in Vermont. That part had not been difficult since all Comcarriers were under constant surveillance. The directives they brought weren't very hard to guess about either; all the National Security Agency had done was wait and watch, ultimately the local communist-party activist — called a drone — would change some tactic, perhaps in the way he set up his college protest demonstrations, or in the way he purged a few members. Finally, NSA was confident that some kind of written, signed document had to pass from Comcarrier to Drone, because the entire Apparatus was a vast bureaucracy. Word-of-mouth might suffice in small details, but like all bureaucracies, the Apparatus throve only on paperwork and signatures. It was also known that large amounts of U.S. currency were carried by Comcarriers from time to time. The Apparatus within the States had never been able to generate its own capital; that may have been a result of its scorn of the capitalistic system, but Pete Waltham thought it more likely the result of the kind of people who were in the Apparatus being unable to successfully compete.

Comcarriers had from time to time been picked up. NSA could have rounded up the entire lot if it had wanted to. The trouble with that, of course, would have been that the Apparatus would have run in an entire new lot, and locating, cataloguing and watching would have to start all over again. When a Comcarrier *was* picked up, it was only done so that NSA could verify its own deductions.

The village of Hamilton, while hardly the ideal spot for contacts — a big city would have been much better — nevertheless was being used. Waltham thought this was a temporary measure; that if anyone within the Apparatus got wind of his presence there, orders would swiftly be sent along to change to some other place. That could even happen anyway, on the basis that, like the bear that never slept more than three nights in one place, if points of contact changed often enough, the pursuit would be thrown off. Which it would be, of course.

Hamilton had several obvious advantages. It was off the beaten track, even for holidaymakers. It was quite accessible to the Canadian border, where Comcarriers arriving from Europe could slip over, deliver, and slip back with a minimum of risk, and finally, it had evidently been a safe 'drop' or contact-point for several months.

All of these things were in the report Waltham glanced through. What was lacking, however, was that one essential: the local contact. Finding him — or her — was a little like being a hunter stalking a tiger, who in turn is wary and experienced enough to also be watching for the hunter whom he knows cannot be very far distant.

Waltham was working under one immediate disadvantage in a place like Hamilton: Somewhere in the village was a person highly sensitive to strangers, and Waltham was a stranger. He would be under someone's eye all the time that he was also trying to guess which person it was.

To mitigate this, NSA's chief had worked out a plausible cover. Peter Waltham had been released from a Massachusetts hospital the previous month, recovering from nervous exhaustion. The cover of course went further: There was a job with a computer manufacturing company complete to faked papers proving seniority, an apartment where he had 'lived' for four years, and even a contrived love affair with a woman who had jilted him, all of it making a reasonably normal background for the Peter Waltham who had never existed.

This also served another purpose. Anyone discreetly checking back on Pete Waltham would be detected doing so, which would not only serve as a warning to Pete but would also, hopefully, supply a clue to the person in Hamilton instituting such an investigation.

No one had undertaken any such investigation as yet. Pete had been almost ten days in Hamilton and for all the good he'd accomplished might just as well have been back home in Quantico, Virginia.

And eventually his cover would go stale. After all, someone recuperating from a nervous breakdown must eventually recover. Of course the nature of his supposed ailment made recovery very elastic from person to person, but notwithstanding he would have to recover sometime.

Stalemate, he told himself, closing the folder and returning it to its hiding place in the room. The riddle was far more sophisticated than it had seemed. NSA had alerted him twice and nothing had come of it in either case. Once, when a Comcarrier with an Interpol tail had landed from Europe in Montreal and had been followed down to the Canadian border where Waltham was supposed to pick him up, and he'd dropped from sight, and again when an Apparatus man from Philadelphia had come north to Hamilton, with an NSA tail this time, and had vanished in thin air before Pete had even got close.

It was good, whatever it was, this

Apparatus system operating out of a nondescript little New England village. Very good. So good Pete Waltham was less intrigued with locating his person — his 'principal' — than he was in knowing exactly how the system had been devised and how it functioned.

He left the hotel for a drive through the late-day heat, which he'd made a practice of doing since coming to Hamilton, nodded and waved to old Doctor Clancy whom he saw standing in the shade on a quiet intersection, window-shopping, and afterwards gently smiled, for it had been through Doctor Clancy that his 'trouble' had been discreetly advertised to the village. He'd gone to see Doctor Clancy his second day in town as though he were a person habituated towards dependency upon medical practitioners.

Clancy, white-headed, ruddy, quite handsome in fact with his twinkling blue eyes and quick smile, had told Pete exactly what Waltham had known he'd say.

'I'm just a small town general practitioner, son. Of course I've read books on

21

psychiatry, but any prescription I'd offer would be based on what you can figure out for yourself: For nervous disorders get plenty of rest, eat heartily, and do whatever excites you the least.' Clancy had then laughed. 'We could start out by going to lunch together.'

Doctor Clancy was a splendid old man in Waltham's opinion. He'd had one small twinge of conscience about using him. But when a person operates under a cover it is necessary, in fact it is *mandatory*, that he use someone to establish the facts of his faked existence.

Northward, Vermont was rolling country. Wilder in appearance than the old, tamed, but also beautiful Virginia countryside. The forests had long ago vanished from Virginia but Vermont still had them. Usually though, they survived only on mountainsides; the valleys, large and small, had long since been cleared and planted. Predominant colour of Vermont farm buildings was red, predominant shade of planted fields was green, dark or pale and betwixt, but green. It helped that summer rains came occasionally too, for otherwise the countryside would have been dry now and parched.

Pete Waltham had never been on assignment in Vermont before. In fact in any capacity whatever, he'd never before visited the postage-stamp-sized state. He liked it even though he was no great admirer of snow, and there was plenty of evidence on all sides that snow came early, piled deep, and stayed late, in this part of the country. It was only August and already there was a nip in the air at night.

He took a little crooked lane and had a pleasant and leisurely drive past, among other things, a pumpkin field where great orange orbs stood at random amid tangles of failing vines, and a gaunt old two-storey farmhouse with a very ornate lightning-rod on top of it, that must have been standing for two hundred years.

He knew a girl in Washington who spent weekends scouring the rural areas around Foggy Bottom for suitable scenes to paint. He thought she would go wild up here around Hamilton.

A dog chased his car once and another

time a gaggle of bellicose geese crossing from a pond on one side of the road to a farmyard on the other side raised wings and made low sidewards passes at him as he went slowly past, hissing their disapproval. A man standing near the house leaned on a spade to watch, and afterwards waved.

Pete waved back.

Finally, threading his way back towards town as the sun dropped to within a yard or two of a pine-spiked mountain rim, he came as close to Hampton House as any road, excepting the private lane of course, allowed one to get, and went slowly along admiring the big old pile of New England stone. It was no Hampton Court, from which he speculated its name might have derived, but for New England it most certainly was a very impressive monument to an historic past.

He grinned, thinking of that weary euphemism people parodied so much now. 'Like New York City, a nice place to visit but I wouldn't want to live there'.

Not much chance, he concluded, and picked up speed a little, completing the big circuit and making the chilly drive through the last mile of forested countryside — part of the Hampton estate — to the outskirts of Hamilton again, his timing excellent because it was now supper time and he was hungry.

At the hotel he showered, re-dressed, then sauntered down to have dinner at the adjoining café — Hamilton's most popular eatery, evidently, because he'd noticed a few days back that Saturday night the merchants brought their families there.

He knew most of them. Hamilton was a small town, he'd made a point of making purchases in its stores. It was the best, in fact, in small towns it was the *only*, way to cultivate the indigenous charm.

3

A Small Suspicion

For Doctor Walter Lee the drive up from Boston was exhilarating, except at Christmas time when regardless of the herculean efforts of the Road Departments of the States he had to pass through, every highway was as lethal as black ice could make it for car drivers.

In August, however, the drive was quite pleasant. He'd made it twice, the first time with a radiologist — female — with whom he kept rather steady company down in Boston, the second time alone because the radiologist couldn't squeeze another holiday out of the Administration Section.

He had said, 'You can't win them all,' and her wistful reply had been: 'I don't; I just want to win one.' She'd topped it with a kiss.

He was recalling that pleasant parting

on the drive back from the Moffit place where he'd been begged to look in on a sick child — diagnosis: mumps: child's age, seven years. Ideal time for males to have mumps — and from time to time reaching to massage his calf where a goose had fiercely assaulted him, pinching hard, and in consequence almost came round the bend so swiftly he could have climbed up the back of a car on ahead which was creeping along. That sort of thing shakes people up even more, at times, than actually participating in a smash-up. In Walter's case it also angered him. He raised a heavy hand to hit the horn and brought it away only after a considerable struggle.

Neither the car up ahead, nor its driver, was familiar to Walter. No need, really, that they should be, for while he'd grown up around Hamilton and knew everyone, he'd been down in Boston to school four years, and since then had almost completed his internship of another two years, living away from Hamilton for nearly all that time.

Newcomers had arrived. Not very

many it was true, but still, the person up ahead on the narrow and rutted county back road was one.

There was no need for haste, actually. The afternoon was waning but it wasn't chilly, and even when he got home he'd have a long wait before dinner. He finally resigned himself to the pace of the car ahead, thinking the stranger had every right to drive slowly, to enjoy the lovely scenery. He even turned now and again to admire it also, for regardless of how many times over the years he'd seen it, Vermont was still his favourite state.

Finally, the driver up ahead happened to glance in his rear-view mirror, saw Walter patiently poking along back there, and dashed ahead a hundred or so yards to a lay-by where he stopped and climbed out.

He was a fairly tall man, youngish, with the build and shoulders of a wrestler, but with a pleasant and open face that grinned ruefully as Walter pulled over and paused.

'Sorry,' said Special Agent Waltham. 'I

was day-dreaming and didn't look back.'

Walter laughed. 'I know the feeling. I thought at first it might be car trouble.'

'No, although I appreciate your stopping.'

Walter considered a moment, then switched off his motor and pushed out a thick hand. 'I'm Walter Lee.'

Waltham said his name, pumped the extended hand, then turned on the charm. He knew who Walter Lee was, and he thought he just might be able to use him, but their encounter had been too sudden; Waltham hadn't evolved any modus operandi as yet in any case. These things made it possible for him to lean there being friendly and casual, and natural.

'Just another holiday maker, I'm afraid, up here to soothe a frazzled spirit.'

'Boston?'

'No. New York,' smiled Waltham. 'You . . . ?'

'Native. I live in Hampton House, that mound of mossy granite on down the road a bit. Well, I shouldn't say I *live* there. My parents do and I *did*, but I've

29

been down in Boston almost six years now. Medicine.'

'Oh,' said Pete Waltham. 'Medicine. Well, as a matter of fact it was medicine that sent me up here. Nervous breakdown with a prescription for a long rest in — '

'Some quiet, dull, unexciting place.' Walter laughed. 'You are to be commended on your choice.'

They both laughed, then Walter's eyes raked over the other man's powerful build and steady eyes. 'You're certainly a picture of health now, Mister Waltham.'

'Hamilton has agreed with me.'

Walter smiled, switched the key and said, 'Good. I'm glad. Well, I hope to see you around.'

As the car pulled away Pete Waltham stood thoughtfully watching it. Now he had an *entrée* to Hampton House, a shaky one but nonetheless a valid one. Nervous people needed doctors the way devout people needed ministers. Probably more so.

Climbing back into the car he thought it had been a stroke of genius to concoct that cover for him. Or luck. On the other hand he had no idea of ever having to use Walter Lee.

For Walter, the interlude had been pleasant in two ways. Waltham looked about as fit as a man could be, so Vermont had agreed with him. Additionally, he had been a pleasant, candid person, worth knowing. In fact, when Walter arrived home he told his parents of the meeting — while he massaged the bruised calf of his leg where Moffitt's dratted goose had pinched him.

Two days later, on his way through the village heading back towards Boston, Walter met Pete Waltham again. This time it was as accidental as before. Walter stopped to have the car filled up at Tony Murphy's station, and at the opposite fuel pump Waltham was sitting in his car with old Horace Clancy. Walter jumped out and strode over, lifted his hand in salute and smiled as the other men greeted him.

'Watch him,' Walter said to Waltham, jerking a thumb towards Clancy. 'He'll get into your pocket-book up to the elbow.'

Doctor Clancy laughed. 'When I was

studying medicine,' he retorted, 'we were content to concentrate on the science. Nowadays you have to also take courses in doctor-patient relationships, so you'll be able to find out how much a man makes so you can bill him accordingly.'

Pete Waltham arbitrated. 'Doctor Clancy, money isn't any good if you're not around to spend it. Doctor Lee, what happens to places like Hamilton when everyone is some kind of specialist?'

Walter gave a little shrug. 'There'll always be general practitioners, Mister Waltham. In fact, I guess you could almost say they'd be the real specialists. By the way, Doctor Horace, that youngest Moffitt boy has the mumps. They tried to telephone you yesterday but couldn't make the connections, so they asked me to come round.'

Clancy nodded. 'Timmy,' he said. 'It's the right time for him to have 'em. Well, Doctor, what did you prescribe?'

Walter grinned. 'Rest, keep warm, plenty of sleep.' It was a private joke; once, during has third year in medical school, Walter Lee had come home to tell

Clancy what had always before seemed to Walter a pretty general evasion, that business of always prescribing rest, food and warmth for every ailment under the sun, was exactly what the terribly knowledgeable and lofty instructors at med school also advised prescribing, although they used a far more sophisticated way of saying it.

Waltham understood, at least he thought he did, so when old Doctor Clancy said, 'Depending upon the nature of the ailment, you can also prescribe water,' Waltham laughed along with the other two.

Then Doctor Clancy said, 'Walter, Mister Waltham here has become interested in our community. I was going to show him that old drawing in the museum of Hampton House's floor-plan.'

Walter made a wide gesture. 'By all means.' He looked at Waltham. 'If you get carried away by that business of the secret passages I can tell you that my father and I once tore out a wall where one of the vaults was supposed to be. It cost a thousand dollars to repair the wall, my mother was angry for a month — and there was no hidden room at all. Otherwise though, the old plan is pretty accurate.'

The attendant came over to say Walter's vehicle had been serviced. He smiled in parting, clapped old Doctor Clancy on the arm, then said, 'Good health, gentlemen,' and went back to his own car.

As he drove away he smiled indulgently. First off, newcomers were attracted to Hampton House, visually; it sat up there on its low roll of clearing like an ancient castle. Secondly, when they visited the local museum and saw that old floor-plan, they were fascinated at the prospect of genuine secret rooms. Finally, with actually very little else around town to hold their interest, they usually listened to the old stories, mightily exaggerated and splendidly re-embroidered down the centuries.

As he reached the main turnpike he wondered what people around Hamilton would do if Hampton House were ever torn down. The answer seemed obvious.

They'd still go on telling the tales of Revolutionary days, pointing to the low hill where Hampton House had stood, and perhaps its absence would blend with the fiction.

It wasn't the only residence dating back to the Rebellion or before, but it most certainly was the most spectacular.

There was a big old hole beneath the Hamilton Hotel — which, incidentally, during the Rebellion, had still been a hostelry, although the original building had long since burned — where local people had manufactured a mighty poor grade of gunpowder for the Continental Army. As a boy Walter had visited the old cellar twice, but never a third time because, apart from being damp and chilly and altogether fearsome, there'd been bats down there that had put the fear of God into him.

There was also, but equally unavailable for casual sightseers, a stone-and-mortar dungeon under the Methodist-Episcopal Church on Third Street which had been where Loyalists had been incarcerated after the war broke out. In fact, the original great oak door with its iron reinforcements, was still intact down there.

In time, Walter mused, heading swiftly down the turnpike, Doctor Clancy would show those things, and others equally hoary, to Peter Waltham, providing Waltham showed the interest, because old Horace Clancy's hobby was such memorabilia. Well, he'd been a widower a good many years, and at sixty-plus it was natural enough for people to look backwards rather than forwards.

Walter speculated briefly about Peter Waltham, and again it struck him, strictly as a medical practitioner, that for someone recently recovered from nervous disorders, Waltham was a splendid specimen of healthy masculinity.

Of course, outward physical appearances had little enough to do with inward mental stresses. Nonetheless, there were — and he should remember, he'd only very recently completed groundwork-studies on it — the physical manifestations of inner tightness; the tics, the unconscious movement of hands, eyes, feet; even the sometimes breathlessness of speech.

Waltham had none.

By evening, Walter had come to a conclusion that seemed, even to him, to be bordering on the ridiculous. Nonetheless, when he had the time, the privacy and the means — a telephone in his apartment — he telephoned down to New York General Hospital and asked about the neuroses of one Peter Waltham.

The first thing that happened was a very long delay before he got any specifics; inordinately long, in fact, considering he was paying for the long-distance call. The second thing that happened was that the resident physician he spoke to down there made him spell his name, give his affiliation with Massachusetts General, and even his home address, before he would confirm that a Peter Waltham had indeed been a patient of their psychiatric department slightly more than a month back.

Walter, annoyed at the delay, the little inquisition he'd been subjected to, rang off full of disgust towards both New York General, and himself.

Later, he brightened up when his local friendly radiologist called and in her most alluring tones invited him over for a late and intimate little supper, with Chianti. After that he forgot all about Peter Waltham.

4

Scuttled Again

Pete Waltham got a signal on Tuesday, two days after he and Doctor Clancy had made the rounds of the old town.

A Comcarrier would arrive at Montreal airport at six o'clock the following morning. His tail this time was not an Interpol agent but a British security man who had been on his way to Washington anyway, and who had been re-routed through Montreal, Quebec, and finally, Washington.

The description of the Comcarrier was simply a number. Six. Waltham had memorised the likenesses of ten known users of the Montreal-Hamilton route prior to arriving in Hamilton. Number six was an Italian. The man would hardly be able, even if a car were waiting in Montreal, to reach the international boundary before Waltham, taking all the time he wished, got up there first.

But he had no intention of going that far north. He would wait north of Hamilton a couple of miles, pick up Six when he passed, and hopefully stick to him like a leech. Hopefully.

When he'd got the signal he'd also been asked if he would like to have two more agents in to help. Not, the Chief hastily exclaimed, because the Agency wasn't perfectly aware of the difficulties, and wasn't entirely satisfied that Waltham would ultimately crack the thing, but simply in order to double up on the percentages.

Peter had declined. 'Two strangers in here now would blow the whole thing, and maybe even blow my cover as well. The people accept me now. The village medic and I are pinochle-playing cronies. Just be patient.'

The Chief had agreed in his customary corn-husk-dry tone to be patient, but afterwards when Waltham went out to eat he wasn't deluded. Unless he turned up something soon, he'd get help. He wouldn't like it, but he most certainly would get it.

Wednesday morning he drove in a leisurely way out of town, southward-bound. It was early; he had plenty of time to make the huge, doubling-back circuit, and get into position before Six came along.

He had binoculars, a zoom-camera, and of course his belt-gun, which he didn't anticipate using. Which, in fact, he'd never had to use yet in any of the cases, or any of the years, he'd worked.

He had nothing against guns at all. A gun was one of those handy things, like a car or a plane, or for that matter a pair of trousers; just because you owned one didn't mean you burned to use it, or even *had* to use it except upon those rare and usually fateful occasions when there was absolutely no suitable substitute.

What Pete Waltham didn't like about belt-guns was that they made his trousers sag.

He checked the road-map, checked the time, did some simple arithmetic, decided Six would pass within the next hour or so, and composed himself for the wait by reflecting upon the interesting historic things he had seen with Doctor Clancy, including that splendid old oak door beneath the Methodist-Episcopal Church. He hadn't seen the old gunpowder magazine beneath the hotel. It was no longer accessible according to the hotel owner; too risky having people go down there, his insurance didn't cover accidents occurring *beneath* the premises, only *on* them, and anyway one of the walls had caved in littering the place with rock shards.

It didn't matter.

A half hour passed. Well ahead of Waltham's estimate and unavoidable because only fourteen cars and trucks had passed previously, which made him noticeable, Six cruised past looking on ahead where Hamilton was clearly discernible in its beautifully picturesque setting.

Waltham didn't get a chance to get a zoom-photo. He didn't even get a chance to reach for the binoculars. One moment he saw the car approaching, the next moment, after he'd recognised his man, the car had passed.

He wanted to jump right out after it but training forbade that. And fortunately, because the next car along carried a man Waltham knew at once as Three, a Comcarrier Waltham had tailed right down to the outskirts of town, and had then lost completely and had never seen again until this moment.

It was not customary for two Comcarriers to travel this close. It was also obvious that Three had not crossed the Atlantic with Six. Otherwise he'd have been signalled about that.

But why?

As he finally eased out of the sideroad and started towards Hamilton it occurred to him that if Six were carrying an immense amount of cash, or was transporting some highly confidential information, it would explain Three's following after like a bodyguard. It also made Waltham push down hard on his accelerator so he could keep both cars in sight, but primarily the car which Six was driving.

Near the outskirts of Hamilton, where

he'd previously turned off on his previous pursuit to avoid being noticed, intending to pick up his quarry again further along, and had never again seen the Comcarrier, this time he dropped back to let an oncoming car pass him and settle into the line behind Three, but he did nothing otherwise that would cause him to lose sight of his men.

Hamilton was three blocks long with the business district, that is, the *major* business establishments such as the bank, drug store, main commercial establishments, occupying the middle block, while lesser businesses occupied the other two streets, on both sides of the road. There was always traffic here, but it was at its peak, it seemed to Waltham, between noon and three o'clock in the afternoon. Not only townsmen, but farmers as well, filled sidewalks, parking sites, and the roadway. Today was no exception, and although he had to yield to several more cars inside the city limits, Waltham was still watching Six up ahead, and Three a car or two behind Six.

They passed the first square then Six

slowed as he entered the second square, swerved and headed for an empty parking area. Waltham wasn't caught unprepared, but he nonetheless had to cruise help-lessly past because there was not another parking slot anywhere around. He watched Six leave his car and stride briskly across to the hotel.

Three turned off on a side avenue seeking a parking place. Waltham stayed with him and when Three had left his car, Waltham had no difficulty cruising on a short distance to a parking place of his own. He then walked back to pick up Three's trail, which wasn't hard because Three had gone into a café and Waltham could see him through the window.

He strolled along to the hotel, satisfied that if he couldn't watch them both he most certainly could keep one of them in sight all the time, and Six being the one he'd been alerted about, he'd watch that one.

There was no one in the musty lobby when he entered. The elderly man at the registration desk, called Tom by everyone, looked a little like Horace Clancy with his white thatch, ruddy complexion and pleasant glance. He nodded at Waltham, who went over and leaned on the desk to smilingly ask how business was.

Tom laughed as though at an old joke. 'Business is boomin',' he replied. 'Last week we had seven salesmen spend the night passin' through, and you of course, but so far this week we ain't had a soul. Now I'd say that's right busy, wouldn't you?'

Waltham blinked. 'No one at all this week, Tom?'

'Nary a soul.'

'But . . . ' Waltham took a long chance. 'But . . . a man asked me across the street just a few minutes ago if you would have any vacancies and I sent him over. I saw him walk in.'

Tom considered that briefly, then brightened. 'Well, yes, there was a feller. Swarthy-like he was.' Tom grinned wide. 'Maybe he wanted a room, but he asked me if we had a ground floor johnny and I pointed to the door there. That's the room he went into.'

Waltham turned, surveyed the closed

door with the worn gold lettering that said, 'Gentlemen', turned back and tried to match old Tom's twinkling glance as he shrugged. 'Maybe he fell asleep, Tom. Well, I did my good deed for the day so I'll sit here a minute and relax.'

Tom pointed. 'There's the morning papers, Mister Waltham. Kind of rumpled; we got a few local fellers come in here every danged morning to sit and read our papers, and leave 'em rumpled like that.'

Waltham crossed to a chair that faced the lavatory door, sat, picked up one of the rumpled papers and started his vigil. Not until something like fifteen minutes later when Tom came over and said, 'You don't reckon that feller really *did* fall asleep in there, do you?' did he put aside the paper and rise with a sinking feeling in the pit of his stomach. He thought he knew what had happened, but he couldn't explain to himself *why* it had happened. He'd been especially careful that neither of the Comcarriers should suspect they were under surveillance.

He went to the closed door, knocked

lightly, then opened the door. The bathroom was empty with a very slight breeze rustling some old lank curtains on each side of the opened window.

He had guessed right — too late.

He still couldn't imagine what had made Six go to all this elaborate trouble to cover his tracks, unless he'd either seen Waltham or had suspected he was being watched.

Tom said, 'Be damned. I didn't see him come out of here, Mister Waltham, but he sure must have, eh?'

Waltham agreed that the stranger surely must have left the lavatory, crossed the empty lobby, all unnoticed, and got loose of old Tom to walk back outside, where he headed directly over across the street to a position where he could see into the café through its large roadway window.

To his enormous relief Three was still in there having his luncheon.

Now, Waltham moved only as far as he had to in order to be able to keep up a discreet vigilance. Twice people strolled past whom he knew and smiled at. One

48

was Doctor Clancy on his way to a young woman having pains with her first child.

'I'll walk out there,' complained Clancy, 'in the confounded heat, then it'll turn out she's been eating green apples or something. Mister Waltham, you'd be surprised how easy it is for women to agitate themselves into false labour pains.'

Clancy went on, while across the street Three had a second glass of iced-tea and lit a cigarette while he turned to making a very slow and careful study of the town.

Waltham was sure of one thing; somewhere in this nice, drowsy, picturesque little New England village, Six and someone else were sitting down in seclusion transacting their business.

Of course all wasn't lost at all, for apart from having Three in sight, Waltham would get another chance if and when a Drone showed up to pick up whatever Six had left behind.

It was, he told himself consolingly, as much as he was expected to do, in any case. Of course the answer that came to mind the moment he thought this, was not quite so consoling. He was supposed, also, to discover who, where, and how, this transaction between Six and someone else was accomplished.

Three finished his smoke, his iced-tea, and arose to smilingly pay his tab, then stroll out into the afternoon heat. He took his time about returning to the parked car, climbing in, and lighting another smoke. He neither started the car nor seemed in any hurry to depart at all, so Waltham thought he was either stealing a little time off, now that he'd delivered his companion safely, or else that he just might be waiting for Number Six to come along with his fresh instructions. In either case, Waltham kept watch on both the car and the man sitting in it leisurely smoking, from an ideal vantage point — the sympathy-card counter of the local gift shop.

After almost a half hour Number Three finally did something Waltham hadn't anticipated; he reached into a holster suspended beneath his right shoulder, drew forth a small transceiver, put it to his ear as though listening, then, he lowered it to speak.

Waltham left the store quickly and went heading for the next block where Six had parked his car prior to entering the hotel. It was gone.

He wanted to swear. Instead he smiled at a darkly handsome woman he knew was Mrs Frank Lee, then turned and with exaggerated slowness strolled back to look round where Number Three had been parked. That car, and its occupant, was also gone!

5

Death Intrudes

The Chief was not a man who normally wasted time consoling people. When he called Pete Waltham up at Hamilton to warn him a Drone name Blavatsky was heading north from Detroit, and Waltham told him of losing Three and Six, all the Chief said was, 'Don't worry about that. You'll have better luck with Blavatsky. But things are about to break anyway, Pete. A man named Walter Lee, Doctor Walter Lee whom we traced to Massachusetts General Hospital in Boston, and who lived most of life with his parents up there, telephoned down to New York General asking about you. That's the first signal we've had and I don't mind saying it was gratefully received. Do you know Lee?'

'I know him,' replied Waltham, 'I won't say I'm altogether surprised, but I *will* say of all the people I've met around here, Walter Lee would be my last choice; his people are wealthy, he's a career medical man. In speaking with him you don't get any feeling at all that he's hungup — no quirks, no neuroses.'

The Chief's tone implied a hint of sarcasm. 'Well, of course he could just be a curious medical man, Pete, but there has to be *someone* up there who is the intermediary. Right now — so far — the only fly that's blundered into any of our traps is Doctor Walter Lee. But what's most important now is Blavatsky. I'll send you the gen on him this afternoon, but for now he's under patrol surveillance and you'll be signalled from the air when he's close to your station.'

Blavatsky was not a familiar name. After talking with Washington, Pete went down to that same café where Number Three had had his luncheon and iced-tea, ordered an early dinner and took his time about eating it.

He wasn't worried about Blavatsky. He'd start worrying when the man arrived, which wouldn't be until sometime the following day. About Three and Six he *did* worry. For one thing he knew the Chief was not pleased. For another Waltham wasn't pleased with himself, either.

But what overshadowed everything else was the identical thought that had been teasing him for two weeks now. Where did these people meet and who was their local contact?

After dinner he managed to meet Doctor Clancy at the local tobacconist's place. They took a small table near the back of the room to play pinochle, and Waltham started his discreet interrogation, something he occasionally did with Clancy because thus far at any rate, Clancy was the only close acquaintance he had in Hamilton, but even more important than that, Doctor Clancy had spent almost his entire professional life here; if he didn't know someone, or hadn't made discoveries concerning their affairs, no one else would know them either.

But Doctor Clancy could be very evasive when he chose to be. Now, concentrating on pinochle, he turned the questions aside deftly. Only after he'd won their first game easily did he light a pipe, call for a glass of beer, and respond to the queries concerning the Lee family.

They were fine people, he told Pete Waltham, and sketched in the family background. He'd known old Kingsley Lee, and about him Clancy was both direct and tart. But the elder Lee had been dead a long time now.

About Frank and Emily Lee he spoke fondly. When it came to Doctor Walter Lee his information dried up about when he told of Walter going down to live in Boston, which of course was the part Waltham was most interested in.

He could have the Agency run a check on Walter easily enough. In fact, after hearing what the Chief had told him that same afternoon, he was confident the Agency was already hot-footedly doing just exactly that. No doubt, when the information arrived on Blavatsky, there would also be something enclosed on young Lee.

But that wasn't what Waltham was after. The Agency couldn't look inside a man's mind simply by digging up his statistics. It was necessary to *know* a person in any ideological conflict to understand what he could, or would, do.

Then Clancy said something that altered Waltham's attitude for the balance of the evening. 'You're pretty interested in the Lees, Peter, aren't you?' Clancy the trained observer, was looking squarely at Waltham through a pale and fragrant mist of pipe tobacco.

'I'm interested in *Hamilton*, Doctor. You know that by now. Not just one person who lives here — or who used to live here — the whole lot of you.' Waltham smiled as Clancy's beer arrived. 'I may be around here for a long time, Doctor. I like it very much. So I'm interested.'

Clancy tasted the beer, smiled and said, 'You ought to have some of this, it's very good.'

Waltham had a glass and another game of pinochle. The beer *was* good, and Doctor Clancy trounced him again at pinochle, then, as he walked the older man home through a full-moon night,

Clancy said something else.

'I'll let you in on a secret . . . No; I'll make my point with a story. Once there was this physician who was getting old. He sent away for a younger physician to come and succeed him. But first he took the younger man on the rounds with him. The younger man agreed with each diagnosis the old man made, except one. That was when the old doctor told a sick woman that along with cutting down on sweets, she must also stop going to church. The young physician said he didn't see that going to church had anything to do with the woman's condition. The old physician said the reason he'd made that prescription was that he'd seen the local minister's shoes under the woman's bed.'

Waltham laughed. Clancy looked up at him with a twinkle. 'Maybe that doesn't make my point very well, but you see, Pete, physicians are schooled to be observant. In both our games of pinochle tonight you could have beaten me — if your mind had been on the game. Well, here we are. I'm obliged for you seeing me home. Goodnight.'

Back at his room in the hotel Pete shook his head. He was amused. He was also mildly alarmed. He didn't believe a man of Clancy's benign philosophy would be involved with Comcarriers, but of course that wasn't the point. What mattered was that Clancy was suspicious of him, and *that* could be fatal, if old Clancy mentioned his doubts around town, because inevitably the unknown intermediary would hear about it.

It was always good to have a local ally, but the Agency was purposefully vague about this; it did not like the idea of outsiders being taken into even limited confidence even though every special agent knew local friends were very often the difference between success and failure.

In this particular case Waltham's need for a local assistant was not as essential, yet, as his need to know who the local intermediary was, and where this person was making his contacts.

It was somewhere in town, obviously; Six hadn't climbed out that lavatory window to go to any very distant rendezvous. If he had, of course, some of the clanny local people would have noticed him as a stranger right away.

Waltham retired thinking he would start a discreet enquiry the next morning about that, and fell asleep.

He had not resolved the thorny question of making a confidant out of old Doctor Clancy, but when he awakened in the morning two simultaneous ideas occurred. One was that Doctor Clancy, the observant medical practitioner, had probably been studying Waltham while Waltham was also studying Doctor Clancy, and the advantage lay with the older man. He would very likely know there was nothing wrong with Waltham. *How* he would know this Waltham wasn't prepared to say; he was not a physician. But he had that feeling and it persisted.

The second thought was that, since Walter Lee and Clancy were old friends as well as fellow practitioners, it was just possible Clancy might contact young Lee, or vice versa, to discuss Peter Waltham.

What this amounted to, of course, was

that Pete Waltham's involvement was nearing some critical phase. He went down to breakfast believing this and when he returned old Tom at the desk called him over to get a letter that had arrived with the morning post. He took it upstairs.

There was, as he'd anticipated, a hastily typed report on Walter Lee, evidently worked up after the talk with the Chief. Otherwise, the letter contained the Blavatsky report, and along with that, two photographs, one close up and head-on while the man was standing at a bus-stop in a crowd, and again when Blavatsky seemed to be giving some kind of address, although there was very little of the audience in the picture — just the backs of several long-haired heads.

The man's first name was Otto, which Waltham thought was a fair contrast of names, German and Russian, and his age was given as forty-four, his marital affiliation as dissolved, and his general background as a hard-liner. He had been dismissed as a political science instructor at a Catholic college.

Waltham grimaced. The mystery would be — how did a Catholic board of regents ever *hire* such a man? Blavatsky was a dedicated and lifelong Apparatus-man. His record within the Party was excellent, his contacts wide and lively. Currently he was serving as co-ordinator of student activists on the West Coast.

'And that,' said Waltham aloud, 'takes money. Especially now when they've worked up some real donnybrooks out there. So — Six was carrying money, and Three was covering him to make certain he delivered it.'

The obvious next conclusion was that Blavatsky was coming — the trusted Apparatus organiser and upper echelon official — to get that money and take it back to the West Coast with him for rather obvious purposes.

Waltham finished reading, pocketed the letter and went to stand a moment by his front window facing the street. Up to this point everything was going exactly as it usually went. No trouble, no hitches, only a very faint scent of failure.

But that little quaint town down there,

with its historic manor house a half mile off beyond town upon its greensward-hill, was the truly deceptive part. It looked so innocent, like some varieties of snakes, and turned out to be so disastrously poisonous.

The telephone rang and Doctor Clancy was on the line. 'Been an accident down the turnpike and my car's not working too well, Pete, so I was wondering if you could lend me yours.'

Waltham recoiled at once. He'd need that car to use in covering Blavatsky. On the other hand —

'Some damned ninny with an odd name coming up through our country rear-ended a huge cement truck. Some name like Bluvitsky or something; the State Police called a few minutes ago. I'm the nearest medic, you see?'

'Bluvitsky, did you say, Doctor?'

'Well, something like that, Pete. I never could pronounce those Balkan names — or is that one Russian? Blavotsky, Bluvitsky . . . '

'I'll do better than lend you the car, Doctor, I'll be right over to pick you up and we'll both go have a look.'

Waltham rang off, stared at the cradled telephone a moment, then flapped his arms and quietly swore. This damned fool Blavatsky had to go and get himself hurt, which meant the most recent person who could have led Waltham to the Hamilton intermediary would not now be able to do so.

He debated whether to call Washington or not, decided not to just yet, went down and drove over to pick up Doctor Clancy.

It was a beautiful summer day, not hot yet and without a cloud in the turquoise sky. Traffic on the carriageway was heavy, mostly huge lorries carrying inter-state commerce, but also with a goodly number of passenger cars.

When they reached the accident-site a number of police cars with red-flashers blinking, had hemmed-in the immediate area. There was a huge dry-cement truck, with trailer, facing north. Behind it was a demolished private car. A beefy uniformed officer took Clancy and Waltham over to the grassy verge, where Waltham got a shock. Blavatsky was completely covered by a grey blanket.

The policeman halted gazing dispassionately downward. 'I'm sorry, Doctor. We were sure he'd be able to hold on until someone got here. But he didn't.'

Clancy knelt and pulled back the blanket. Waltham recognised the face at once. After a life of dedication to something Blavatsky had undoubtedly believed in whole-heartedly, and which Peter Waltham was just as dedicated in opposing, the end of the trail had come for Otto Blavatsky on the grassy verge of an inter-state highway.

Not a very heroic way for a lifelong revolutionary to cash in his chips. In fact, in Waltham's view, it was an altogether unsatisfactory way all round.

He turned and looked at the little knot of people farther back. They were mostly uniformed highway patrolmen, but there was an ashen cement-truck driver and there was also a quietly interested man in everyday-attire examining Blavatsky's demolished vehicle. Waltham strolled over to also look at the car. The other man looked up and said, 'I was going to leave him at the Hamilton city limits. Good thing I didn't leave any sooner. How are you, Pete?'

'Right now, Henry, I'm not so good. What in the hell brought this about?'

'It was Blavatsky's fault. The cement rig was travelling along about forty-five miles an hour and in his own lane. I don't know what Blavatsky was thinking of, but he was moving along at about seventy-five miles an hour. He overtook the big rig, started to swerve past, hooked his right fender with the big rig's left wheel, and although both were travelling in the same direction, Blavatsky, going nearly twice as fast, got the effect of hitting a stone wall at high speed. He shot out through the windshield.' The man shrugged at Waltham. 'Tough luck, eh?'

'Are you going straight back?' asked Waltham.'

'Yes. They've got me tied in as a witness.'

'Do you have a cover?'

'Oh sure. Look in the back of my car over there. I'm a toy salesman out hustling pre-Christmas orders. I'll call the

Chief from the patrol headquarters.'

'Okay.' Waltham sauntered back over where Doctor Clancy was talking to the big uniformed patrolman. When he saw Waltham he smiled at the officer. 'You won't need me any more.'

'No sir, and thanks for responding. I'm sorry it turned out to be a wild goose chase.'

Clancy was quiet as he walked along with Waltham back to their car. As he climbed in he sighed and said, 'A fairly young man too, Pete. Hell of a waste.'

6

A Fresh Arrival

Peter felt no charity towards the dead man. But then if Blavatsky had lived he wouldn't have felt any for him either. But dead he added to the sense of frustration that sent Waltham down to a little tavern on the north edge of town the night after Blavatsky's passing to liquify some of the kinks out of his psyche. It worked. It almost invariably worked.

There, he encountered Armand Dulette, owner of the Hamilton Hotel, and the haberdashery directly across the street from the hotel. Armand was not actually the kind of man Waltham warmed to. He was a distinct type of French-Canadian; one of those with the slightly hooked nose, the black hair and the very dark, alert eyes. He was not a very tall man, slightly below average in fact, but he had once been physically strong and durable.

Now, perhaps near fifty although with his type it was always hard to guess closely, he was running slightly to a paunch and a kind of coarseness around the jowls that detracted from what had once perhaps been a keen and hawklike appearance.

He was a friendly man, but Waltham had always felt as though Armand Dulette's interest was pecuniary, whether he was looking at a building or a man.

He had come to Hamilton seventeen years before, not very long after he'd been discharged from the Canadian army where, or so old Tom at the hotel had told Waltham, he had served with heroism and distinction.

It wasn't hard to believe that about Dulette, but first one had to look past the subcutaneous fat for the lean, hawkish, black-eyed man of seventeen and more years ago.

Tonight he was drinking alone at the counter and eating salted peanuts. When Waltham sat nearby Dulette nodded, smiled, and offered the bowl of peanuts. 'They will kill you. Very high in protein which results in plugging the arteries.'

When Waltham declined Dulette set the bowl back in front of himself and scooped out another big handful which he fed into his mouth a few at a time as he mused aloud.

'Of course no one lives forever, eh, Mister Waltham? And when one thinks about that it's not a very nice prospect anyway, is it? So I eat peanuts. Because I like them. Maybe also because if my arteries get all filled with fat or whatever it is that fills them, I'll only be fulfilling my destiny in any case. What do you think?'

Waltham's drink arrived, a very dry martini. He tasted it, found it agreeable, and said, 'I think, Mister Dulette, that if the philosophers who've kicked this one around since the beginning of time, had built bridges instead, by now we'd be able to walk all the way to Europe.'

Dulette threw back his head and roared with laughter, then he signalled for a second drink and turned around on the bar stool so he could look directly at Waltham.

'That is very good,' he said. 'Now tell

me one more thing: Your conviction respecting death?'

Dulette's drink came but he ignored it. His lively dark eyes remained fixed upon Peter Waltham as though he had just made a remarkable discovery; this young man whom he'd come to know casually at his hotel, and who looked so harmlessly nondescript, all of a sudden was turning out not to be nondescript after all. At least not *mentally* nondescript, and that interested Dulette immensely, for in Hamilton he'd often felt frustrated, drained-dry, rather than stimulated.

Waltham moodily finished his highball and let Armand Dulette hang there, waiting. Every sense Waltham possessed was invariably sharpened by liquor. It was happening now as he waggled a finger at the bartender for a re-fill, and the somewhat casual disinterest rather than dis*like*, he felt for Dulette, hardened sufficiently to affect his present attitude.

And there was another reason why he offered no immediate answer. He had seen death face to face very recently; it did not now, and it never had, inspire him to start speculating about it, right after it had been and gone.

'Well, my friend Mister Waltham . . . ?'

Peter shot a blank look at the older man. 'What does your priest tell you, Mister Dulette? He's the best man for that question anywhere around; he's been living with death all his ecclesiastical life. Me; I've seen my share of it, and it's always the same. Not frightening, exactly, but very unnerving. It is an end to continuity for someone, and being a rational human being, that stuns me. I have nothing to say about death at all.'

'And yet you saw it down on the turnpike, did you not?' Dulette spread his palms as Waltham looked hard at him. 'Old Tom has talked with Horace Clancy. You took Clancy down there and you saw a dead man. That would still be fresh in your mind, no?'

'Of course it's still fresh in my mind. That's a damned-fool question, Dulette.'

'No offence,' murmured Dulette, looking quickly from the near-empty glass in Waltham's hand to his face, both dark eyes showing wonder, and wariness. 'I simply wanted to hear your opinion. You know, for a long while I was a soldier. In a very long war, you understand. Soldiers think of death very much.'

'Okay, Mister Dulette; *you* tell *me*.' Waltham drained his glass, pushed it away and swung to stare at the olive-complexioned hawkish man. 'Shoot, I'm listening.'

Dulette gave a little uneasy laugh. 'Some other time, then, eh?' He examined Waltham's flushed face and kept smiling. 'Have you had dinner, *mon ami*?'

'No. Don't change the subject. You got a big laugh out of me, now let's see you make me laugh.'

Dulette's eyes showed annoyance, but they also still showed wariness. Finally he leaned on the bartop and slowly ran a thick hand along the loose angle of his dark-shadowed jowl. 'There is no pattern, I can tell you that after seeing hundreds of men die, Mister Waltham. It simply plucks away one and does not even see the man right next to the one it comes for.'

'Okay. That sounds good. But I'm not laughing.'

The dark eyes flashed stormily. 'There is nothing about death to laugh about, Mister Waltham. Take that man who died on the turnpike; was he funny?'

'Not very,' assented Waltham, and waved away the bartender. 'Okay, I was out of order about wanting to be made to laugh.'

'You need either black coffee or a hot dinner, Mister Waltham.'

Peter nodded, his eyes stone-steady. 'That's not what I need, but at that it sounds better than staying in bed, drinking lots of water and getting plenty of rest.'

Dulette's forehead furrowed. 'Are you ill, then?'

Waltham finally smiled. 'Nope. Never felt better. That's just an inside joke between old Clancy and young Walter Lee. Do you know young Lee, Mister Dulette?'

'Of course. He grew up here. Nice boy.'

It had an empty ring to it the way Dulette said it and Peter's sharpened senses detected the falseness at once.

'But you don't like him,' he said, and nodded. 'I don't much care for him either. But with me it's just jealousy I guess. I've never been too wild about anyone who inherits the easy life.'

Dulette looked up. 'No? You are a socialist then, eh?'

Waltham shrugged, picked out some peanuts and ate them.

'I'm a nothing, Mister Dulette. I just don't like people who get born with silver spoons around.'

'You don't like the system then, eh?' said Dulette, his black eyes brightening again, turning fiercely piercing. 'Let me tell you something, Mister Waltham; the system made that suit you wear, it created that car you drive, and it gives you the money in your pocket that you spend in here tonight.' Dulette got off his stool, nodded goodnight and walked out of the tavern.

Waltham continued eating peanuts. He hadn't lied about skipping dinner tonight. Moreover, the peanuts were fresh-roasted and quite good to taste.

He'd stung Armand Dulette and that amused him. He didn't care for the man anyway, and that braying big loud laugh of his had grated.

Waltham also departed from the tavern after a while and, feeling much less frustrated, although he wasn't sure he should ascribe this to the drinks or to the pleasure he'd derived from annoying Dulette, went in search of dinner.

After eating, and still enjoying a diminishing sensation of euphoria, he returned to his hotel room, showered and went to bed. It was ten o'clock. At eleven the telephone rang bringing him bolt-upright in his bed.

It was a crisp, authoritative, incise voice from NSA headquarters in Washington and Waltham recognised it immediately as belonging to NSA's number two man, Howard Worthington.

'We've been alerted that another Drone is on his way to Hamilton, replacing Blavatsky. We tried contacting you earlier without much luck.' Worthington let that hang in the air a moment as though awaiting an explanation. When none was forthcoming he then said, 'This replacement is a man named Ellingwood. Thomas Ellingwood. The report on him will be sent to you first thing in the morning, but of course it won't reach you in time, so we have the car licence number.' Worthington gave it. Finally, he said, 'Ellingwood is six feet tall, Pete, and has a finger gone off his left hand. That should help.'

After this call was terminated Waltham got a drink of water then returned to bed, sat a moment shaking his head over the description, and with an oath of exasperation dropped back into bed again.

Someone with a finger off his left hand would hardly be noticeable as he was driving up the turnpike for this particular peculiarity. As for the car number, it would have to suffice. Waltham yawned, turned up on his side and slept.

He awakened to a beautiful summer morning with a golden sun climbing and with the invigorating fragrance of flowering bushes rising to his open window. As he dressed he wondered about Thomas Ellingwood. Although he was at least acquainted with the names of national Comcarriers, and in some cases knew Drones on sight, the name Ellingwood meant nothing to him.

It was very probably an assumed name in any case so he hardly worried as he went down to breakfast. What *did* interest him was the swiftness with which the Apparatus had reacted to Blavatsky's passing. Of course that implied someone, somewhere, needed that money Numbers Six and Three had delivered to Hamilton, and needed it badly. Pursuing this line of reasoning took Waltham to the inevitable next step: The Apparatus had something very special, and evidently very expensive, planned for not too distant in the future.

Waltham had a second cup of coffee. On the West Coast, perhaps? Or perhaps in some fresh sector where the nation could be embarrassed? If Waltham could prevent Ellingwood from getting the money it would help the nation, although strictly speaking his job with the National Security Agency was not to play knight errant, only to observe, to help complete the knowledge of Apparatus methods. Nothing more.

He considered his watch, went out to the car and drove slowly southward as he always did when his destination was northward. Not that he thought he was under surveillance; it was simply habit to react first, then to act.

It was a long drive but a very pleasant one. By the time he'd threaded his way back northward over back-country lanes and emerged upon the turnpike, it was midmorning. By the time he'd cruised for two hours, or until slightly past high-noon, he was more than a hundred miles southward along the turnpike, and that was when he picked up the memorised licence number coming towards him.

He had only a glimpse of Thomas Ellingwood, hardly enough to define anything, but he was nevertheless sure he did not know the man by sight.

He had to cruise another four miles before encountering an off-ramp that permitted him to reach a state roadway below, which in turn took him beneath the turnpike and up the opposite on-ramp. Then he was heading back towards Hamilton in the same lane, but miles behind, Thomas Ellingwood.

He drove rapidly for a half hour, before he recognised the vehicle up ahead, put the binoculars on the licence plate to be certain, and afterwards slowed to a decent cruising speed until he saw Ellingwood turn on his flashing left-turn indicator. Waltham slowed, let the car ahead leave the turnpike by the off-ramp that led in the southerly direction towards Hamilton, let Ellingwood get well ahead, then Waltham accelerated, and also descended from the turnpike by the same off-ramp.

After that he had to be more discreet. The state carriageway, only two lanes, and not nearly as well-travelled, was level and straight right to Hamilton's outskirts; it would be no great chore for someone wary of being followed to determine that in fact there really was someone far back watching him.

Waltham had solved that on his previous pursuits. He solved it the same way now — by allowing Ellingwood to reach the outskirts of the village well in the lead. From there on Waltham knew about which procedure would be followed anyway; they'd all followed it.

7

Success, Finally

Thomas Ellingwood slowed to a crawl as he entered Hamilton, not, Waltham was sure, because he wished to reassure himself that he wasn't under surveillance, but because he was entering a strange town and Ellingwood wished no embarrassment from some ridiculous infraction of local law.

It was always the nightmare of people operating beyond the law, or operating in secret, that something stupid and accidental would destroy them. They were trained for all predictable exigencies. It was the accidental occurrence that they dreaded most.

Waltham profited by Ellingwood's exaggerated caution by nipping down the first intersecting sideroad, cutting quickly round the square and emerging in a direction that faced the snail-paced, oncoming vehicle.

Ellingwood was already easing into a parking slot a square away, and this time Fate seemed to be on Waltham's side because he too found a suitable place to pull to the kerbing, switch off his engine and sit for a moment, Ellingwood in his view several hundred yards northward, but clearly visible.

Waltham saw the other man alight, turn very slowly scanning the business section of town, face towards the nearside kerbing and walk forward. He was not only on the opposite side of the street from the hotel, which Number Six had used in his final dodge to throw off any pursuit, but Ellingwood remained over there, walking northward as though he were not the stranger that he obviously was.

Waltham finally got a fairly close look at the man. Thomas Ellingwood was about six feet tall and weighed in the neighbourhood of two hundred pounds. He was neither a small nor frail man. His features were good, being even and well-spaced. The man's clothing looked expensive.

Waltham thought that if Ellingwood's purpose was to look like a moderately successful salesman on his rounds, he most certainly was succeeding. He also noticed, when Ellingwood was almost abreast of his car upon the opposite side of the street, that the man missed very little; his glances constantly moved, constantly saw this or that. As Peter Waltham lowered his head to escape the oncoming man's glances, he decided that whether he'd ever seen Ellingwood or not in his past work against the Apparatus, he should now make a note to remember the man, for Ellingwood was definitely no novice at what he was about.

Ellingwood strode the full length of the business district, hesitated up there on the farthest corner while he stood watching the other pedestrians, then he swung down a side street and disappeared.

Waltham left his car in controlled haste and hurried down towards the corner where Ellingwood had disappeared. He knew there were a dozen or so small stores around that corner in a westerly direction — a bakery, a cleaning and laundering establishment, a sign-painter, a barber shop, little individual businesses — what troubled him the moment he saw Ellingwood duck around there was that he might disappear again inside one of those small places of business.

But he hadn't. When Waltham got up there and slowed to a casual stroll, turning the corner, he saw his man turn again, this time walking northward, and once again pass from sight as he headed on around the square.

Waltham made a fast decision. He thought Ellingwood was simply making a complete circuit of the square as a final precautionary measure; it would be easy for the man to determine whether he was being followed on a back street where any pedestrians at all were a rarity. Rather than walk into that kind of trap, Waltham retraced his steps, went back almost to his parked car, then crossed to the same side of the street and loitered where he commanded an excellent view of the terminating side street where Ellingwood would emerge, if he were indeed simply taking a precautionary stroll.

Of course it occurred to Waltham he might be mistaken, in which case there was an excellent chance he'd never see Ellingwood again, and in *that* case . . . Waltham didn't even speculate on what would befall him if he lost another one.

Ellingwood came forth into the bright sunshine and Waltham let all his breath out very slowly before taking in another big breath. He became obsessed with a hangnail.

Ellingwood made another of those slow scans of the area, and finally he stepped off the kerbing heading on across towards the hotel.

Waltham took no chance this time. He briskly walked down towards where Ellingwood would enter, if he didn't turn, and enter the hotel from out front. They weren't more than fifteen feet apart when Ellingwood passed on in, hesitated to let his eyes adjust to the gloominess, then went towards the desk where old Tom was standing with his back to the room, reading an opened newspaper.

Luck was still with Waltham. Old Tom

hadn't heard Ellingwood yet, and neither of them had seen Waltham cut diagonally across the lobby to enter the lavatory. He closed the door swiftly, pulled aside the curtains, heaved up the window and hoisted himself on through into the alley way beyond. It hadn't taken a moment. He then turned, hauled down the window from outside and paused to consider where to hide.

There weren't too many places, but a nearby shed which seemed upon the verge of imminent collapse from endless winter snows looked inviting. Otherwise there was a broken and sagging picket fence across the alleyway, or a heap of old packing crates flung carelessly from the rear of a general mercantile store some distance northward.

The old shed had a stall where in the previous century someone had undoubtedly kept a horse. It also had a foul odour and layers of diaphanous spider-webs of surprising strength when Waltham blundered into them. But it was exactly right for his purpose. There was enough daylight coming past the warped and shrunken vertical side-boards to allow Waltham to look back without any difficulty.

He saw Ellingwood do exactly as Number Six must also have done; he came through that lavatory window like a man following very minute instructions. Afterwards he paused to wipe his hands on a white handkerchief and very slowly look around at his new surroundings. Finally, pocketing the handkerchief, he moved towards the northerly end of the building, tried a door to a jutting projection Waltham took to be a store-room for the hotel or one of the adjoining businesses, opened the door and disappeared from sight, closing the door after himself.

Waltham stood for almost a further fifteen minutes waiting for Ellingwood to emerge. When there was no sign of this happening, he gave it up, ducked out the back way of his shed and walked hurriedly on around to the main thoroughfare, where, at a more leisurely gait, he returned to the hotel's front entrance, nodded to old Tom at the registration desk as though he hadn't been in earlier, then went up to his room to shed his coat, his hat even his tie, and leaned upon the windowsill gazing down where Ellingwood's car still stood. Finally, he put in a call to Washington and when the Chief came on, alerted to who was calling, Waltham reported exactly what had happened in a very calm tone of voice.

The Chief was interested. In fact, he was piqued, for he said, 'Give me some names and I think we'll be on our way.'

Waltham had to think a moment. He knew the storekeepers around town and mentioned the ones doing business nearest that corner of the building where the supposed storeroom was. His actual interest was not in this aspect at all, and ultimately he said, 'Ellingwood is doubtless going to get that money Six brought.'

The Chief chuckled. 'Fine idea. Don't get in his way, Pete.'

'You will take care of that from your end?'

'You can depend upon that. But it will be stage-managed a damned long way from your position. An accident, perhaps;

we'll come up with something.'

Waltham was sure of that. Next, he said, 'I'll have a look inside that storeroom tonight myself.'

'Is that advisable?' asked the Chief.

Waltham almost swore. 'What is the alternative, sir; sit here and watch them go back and forth in an endless stream?'

'No, hardly that, Peter, but now that we know *where* this drop is, if you'll continue to advise us when a Comcarrier arrives, we'll take pains to see that seemingly unrelated apprehensions are made a long way from Hamilton. I think that may be the answer for us, at least for the time being.'

There was little more to say; prolonged telephone calls were always discouraged by the Agency.

Waltham went out to a late luncheon and afterwards, feeling a tiny bit annoyed about not being allowed to prowl the back-alley storeroom, but also feeling satisfied that finally, after nearly a half dozen false starts, he'd finally made a good connection, he lingered over his meal, then, seeing Doctor Clancy entering the tobacconist's store, went on down there to try and promote a pinochle game.

Clancy smiled amiably from the little scarred bar where he was having a glass of stout. He motioned for Waltham to have the adjoining stool and waved to the barman for two glasses instead of one. Then he turned a bright, blue eye on Waltham and said, 'Picked up an odd bit of information this morning; that Blavinsky chap — or whatever the devil his name was — had been taking amphetamines. Undoubtedly that was what impaired his distance-judgement when he tried to speed around the cement truck. Isn't that surprising? Here is a man of mature middle years doing something as irrational as though he were one of those totally self-oriented college lads. You won't often come across mature people that foolish.'

'Who said he was mature?' murmured Waltham as their glasses arrived. 'Age doesn't necessarily guarantee maturity, does it, Doctor?'

'No. Not any more than faking a

nervous breakdown would, Pete.'

They looked steadily at one another a moment before Waltham picked up his glass and smiled softly. 'Cheers, Doctor.'

'Same to you lad.' After he drank deeply Doctor Clancy put the glass in its sticky puddle and began to gently revolve it. 'No comment?' he asked.

Waltham shook his head. 'No comment, Doctor. Except maybe to say I didn't think you'd be fooled indefinitely.'

'Thanks,' muttered the medical man dryly, and continued to sit, obviously waiting.

Waltham tried a poor joke. 'I'm really casing the local bank.'

Clancy's reply was still dry. 'The thought crossed my mind.'

Waltham grinned, downed the remainder of his stout and nodded for a refill. After the glass had been taken away he said, 'You're joking, of course.'

'No. *I'm* not although *you* may be. But you've been in Hamilton quite a spell now, Pete, and just how long would it take even a schoolboy to case our bank? No, that isn't it.'

'Any other ideas, Doctor?'

Clancy nodded, looking up with his shrewd blue eyes stone-steady. 'One or two. They're a bit far-fetched though. For instance, the other day you knew that dead man out on the turnpike.'

'Did I indeed?'

'You knew him before we even got down there and found out that he was dead.'

'All right. Anything else?'

Clancy said, 'I'm the one who is supposed to be getting the answers, not asking the questions, Pete.'

Waltham smiled, patted the older man's shoulder and swallowed a few times before speaking again. 'It won't be your local bank, so rest easy on that score. As for Blavatsky, you've scored a bull's eye.'

'Go on, Pete.'

'Sorry, Doctor,' replied the younger man, and rose to toss down a few coins for their drink. 'Now how about some pinochle?'

Clancy finished his stout, stiffly rose and shook his head. 'I don't think so,' he said, and started past.

Waltham caught him by the arm. 'Doctor, have a little trust. I'll fill you in when I can, but for now I can't. It's nothing illegal. Now then — pinochle?'

Clancy turned, looked for an empty table, beckoned, and headed for one far back near the rear of the shop. Waltham followed after the medical man smiling gently. This was his Good Day after all.

8

Caught!

He never saw Thomas Ellingwood again, but at seven the following morning he got another signal. Walter Lee was heading for Hamilton. There was no one trailing Lee for a good reason; it was obvious where he was going and Waltham could take over as soon as Lee got there.

The question to be answered was whether he should pick Lee up out on the turnpike and see where he went first, when he got to Hamilton, or whether to assume he'd go directly out to Hampton House.

Waltham chose the turnpike. It was a beautiful day for driving, he rather enjoyed the chase, but most of all he was sitting on a riddle he had been forbidden to solve.

That had bothered him the previous night when he'd stood by the upstairs window watching Hamilton go to bed at ten o'clock. He could have gone downstairs, around back into the alley and had a look inside that storeroom without arousing anyone.

There were some things in NSA work that took a bit of getting used to. It was not, for example, like police detection where a man stayed on one case until it was resolved. With the Agency a man might be sent forth to do nothing more than find out where Comcarriers were meeting. Then he might be pulled back and sent on something totally different while someone else moved in to take over his previous assignment. Quite often, too, there never was any resolvement in the police sense. Now, for example, when the Chief had been informed of the details of the Hamilton rendezvous, he might very well do nothing at all; might let those people go on secretly meeting in Hamilton for years, content to know they were doing that, and equally content to very discreetly exploit that knowledge in other ways.

It was frustrating at times, but it was

never dull. Well, almost never.

Waltham waited for Walter Lee to cruise past and nearly drowsed off from the daytime heat. He had that letter on Ellingwood that had arrived in the morning post to read and re-read, but Ellingwood was already *passé*. As for Walter Lee, Waltham had only his educated hunch, but he'd always played those hunches, and now he didn't really believe Lee was involved.

He was treated to a surprise, however, when Doctor Lee finally appeared, driving moderately, which in itself was unusual; most drivers used the inter-state highway system as though it were a personal and private race course.

Lee had a passenger and the signal from Washington had not mentioned that, which it most certainly would have, had it been known. Obviously, Doctor Lee had picked up his passenger *after* leaving Boston. Unfortunately, the decision had been not to trail him, otherwise something, by now, would have been dug up about his passenger.

It was a girl, Waltham saw that much as

the car went past, but her face had been turned towards the driver, thus away from Waltham, so he got no chance to see her.

It didn't worry him very much as he eased out in pursuit. There was probably a very plausible explanation anyway. As far as he'd heard, Walter Lee was normal in those respects, and very likely the girl was a weekend guest he was taking along to Hampton House. In any event, with several days to accomplish it, Waltham was confident he'd find at least one opportunity to photograph her.

Walter Lee took the off-ramp down to the Hamilton roadway, but as Waltham half-expected, he did not pursue it all the way into the village, but turned off on a secondary road leading directly past the Hampton estate. Waltham went only as far as a little wooded knoll, left his car by the roadside, took the binoculars with him to higher ground and stood a while watching Lee's car. When he saw it slow for the right-hand turn onto the estate road he lowered the binoculars, remained in the fragrant woods a bit longer, then slowly made his way back down towards the car.

Doctor Clancy was leaning upon the bonnet watching him return.

Waltham was surprised, of course, but before he got back down there he looked off to his left, back down the secondary road until he saw the older man's parked car. Then he smiled.

Clancy took time to stuff his crooked-stem old pipe before saying. 'What really kept me from sleeping, you see, was not the bank. It was the riddle of what else was there around Hamilton anyone would possibly want.' While Waltham tossed the binoculars onto the driver's seat and waited, Doctor Clancy lit up, puffed to make certain he'd nestled the tobacco just right, then removed the pipe to lightly tamp the fire with a coarse thumb-pad and raise his shrewd blue eyes to Waltham's face as he spoke again.

'It just never occurred to me it could be Hampton House. Not until I saw you following Walter and Janet.'

Waltham's interest heightened. 'Do you know the girl?'

'Of course. Janet Bothwell, a radiologist from Massachusetts General; they work together; have been keeping company for a couple of years. He'll probably marry her. But the point is, lad, what do I do about you?' Old Doctor Clancy began shaking his head. 'Even if you could rob Hampton House, believe me, that silver and those antiques are just too-well known throughout the New England states. They'd be able to track you down the minute you started selling them.'

Waltham grinned. It was funny, in a way. In another way it wasn't so funny, because now, in order to keep Clancy from doing something awkward, like perhaps going to the local police, which would blow Waltham's cover, he would have to do enough explaining to keep the old man quiet, and there was always great peril in such a course. He liked Clancy, and he trusted him, but on the other hand neither of those things influenced his judgement. It was simply a matter of never telling a secret, hence it could never be endangered.

But now he had to tell it. The

alternative was to ask to be recalled, in which case another agent would be assigned, and the newcomer would have to waste a month the same as Waltham'd had to do, before he could move about the village with any equanimity, and by then the 'drop' would have very probably served its undermining purpose. He opened the door of his car as though to get in.

'Doc, follow me back to town, to my hotel room. I've got a few letters to show you.'

Clancy puffed his pipe and stoically studied the younger man. 'You wouldn't have anything violent in mind would you?' he asked.

'Doc, if I wanted to shut you up I couldn't find a better place than right here. I haven't drawn a gun have I? Just follow me back to the hotel and I'll tell you enough to perhaps allay your suspicions.'

Waltham might have added that he didn't have a gun with him. Instead, he ducked down, got behind the wheel of his car and punched the starter. Doctor

Clancy stood as before, impassively studying him. Then he shrugged, removed the pipe from his mouth and nodded. Neither of them spoke again.

On the drive back to the village Waltham decided how much he'd tell Clancy. It went against the grain to tell him anything, but silence was now only the most awkward of alternatives. He did not believe Clancy would be content with a rough outline, either. He'd played enough pinochle with him to know that Clancy was a shrewd and thoughtful antagonist.

He did have one cheering thought; Doctor Clancy was not a blabbermouth. He might have learned not to be through his medical vocation, or it might just be that he was naturally a person who disliked talking too much. In either case it added up to a pleasant reassurance as far as Waltham was concerned.

Finally, he smiled. The seasoned stalker, with no previous reason — which was no excuse at all — had grown so careless in the performance of his most recent stalk, that a country physician in an old rattle-trap of a car had got behind him unobserved and had stalked *him*. It was funny. The Chief wouldn't think so, neither would any of his co-workers at NSA, but it was still amusing to him.

He reached town with Clancy's old car visible in the rear-view mirror, drove to the hotel parking area, left the car and stood in afternoon's early warmth near to smiling as Doctor Clancy drove up, stopped his bucket-of-bolts, alighted and paused long enough to pound his pipe upon a tyre to shake it clean. Then he walked on over looking thoughtful.

'I'd feel better if we went up to my place to talk,' he said, eyeing Waltham again with that steady chariness.

'The kid with the mumps would interrupt. Or some woman with false labour pains. Doc, I give you my word, you are as safe upstairs as in your own bed.'

'Lead off,' muttered Clancy, stuffing the pipe into a coat pocket, and afterwards letting the hand remain in there.

Old Tom saw them enter and threw up

one hand in a friendly little wave. They marched up the stairs, Waltham in the lead, and when they reached the door, Clancy hung back for Waltham to enter first. He then stepped in, closed the door, waited to be invited to take a chair, and finally removed the right hand from the coat pocket.

He was holding a revolver from which every vestige of blue had long since been rubbed off. It was grey steel with a four inch barrel, and a bore that looked to Waltham as though it could accommodate a cannonball. The gun was obviously quite old, but it was just as obviously very deadly.

Clancy said, 'Talk, lad, and never mind Big Bertha. I doubt if the shells would still go off. I haven't used the thing in thirty years.'

Waltham sat and considered the weapon. Then he smiled. 'You're an honest highbinder, Doc,' he said. 'But I'll just assume they *would* detonate.' He raised a hand to his inside coat pocket. 'I'm not armed, Doc. My gun's in the dresser drawer yonder. I'm only reaching for some letters.'

'Go right ahead.'

Waltham brought out the letters he'd been receiving on Comcarriers and Drones. As he leaned to put them atop the little table near Clancy, he also began his explanation.

It took a half hour just to sketch in his purpose in being in Hamilton, what was involved, and who the strangers were who arrived, remained only an hour or two, then departed.

The longer he talked the more Clancy's expression altered. Finally he shoved the pistol back into his coat pocket and picked up the most recent letter, the one giving the run-down on Thomas Ellingwood. After that, he found the one referring to Otto Blavatsky, and that one for obvious reasons, held his interest longest.

In the end he said, 'Be damned! I had no idea . . . '

Waltham was wry. 'I'd have been worried, Doc, if you *had* had an idea.'

Clancy fumbled round for his pipe and proceeded to load it. Waltham knew he did not smoke very much, and if he was going to light the thing up again almost before it'd cooled from the last bout, Clancy was simply covering up his astonishment, his confusion, by giving his hands this job to do.

'One for the book,' he muttered, between puffs. Then he leaned back and said, 'I thought about taking the town constable with me when I trailed after you this morning. That could have been embarrassing, eh?'

Waltham nodded, gathered up the letters and put them away as he said, 'Do you like Walter Lee for some role in all this, Doctor?'

'Good heavens no, lad. That's preposterous.'

'Doctor, it's *someone*.'

'Well, obviously it is. *I* can't just off-hand come up with any plausibilities, but I most certainly *can* tell you when you're that far off target.'

Waltham nodded gently, unconvinced. Clancy might be a thoroughly qualified observer of the health scene, but that hardly qualified him for the espionage or intelligence scenes.

'That storeroom at the back you mentioned, lad. I've been in there a number of times. It's not a storeroom as you suspect. It's the entrance to that old gunpowder magazine that's been used as a cellar beneath the hotel. When you walk past the door you turn left very sharply and there is the stairway. It's blacker than original sin down there, smells foul too.' Clancy puffed a moment then gave his head a firm wag. 'Must need privacy very badly to be meeting down in that wretched place.'

That wasn't what Waltham was thinking about. Several weeks back when he'd evinced an historical interest in that cellar he'd been told at the hotel the cellar had partially caved in, was dangerous to enter, and wasn't in use.

9

The First Real Suspect

When Washington had contacted him for names of local merchants who might have access to, or use, that room Waltham had thought was a storehouse, he'd neglected to give one particular name. It hadn't occurred to him at the time. Now it *did* occur to him. Armand Dulette. He debated about putting in the call with Clancy sitting there, considered easing Clancy out while he made the call, then decided against that because for the next hour or two he wanted to be right beside Clancy. Until he was personally satisfied Clancy wasn't going to rush off and do something embarrassing.

He put in the call with Doctor Clancy puffing and candidly listening. He was promised Dulette's name would be put through the computers, that whatever came forth would be forwarded at once, and when he put aside the telephone Clancy said, 'It's like something out of a far fetched novel, all this business of shadowy people coming and going. Pete, are you very sure?'

Waltham was sure. In fact, he was positively certain, but Clancy's attitude was neither new to him, nor would Clancy respond immediately to known facts. Surprise, shock, scepticism, whatever anyone chose to call it, invariably left outsiders given their first view of intelligence operations feeling as though they were in an improbable nightmare as onlooking participants.

Give Doctor Clancy a few hours and he'd make all his judgements; would accept what existed, and would decide what his personal course should be. That was precisely why Waltham wanted the doctor with him for the rest of the afternoon.

He had an idea. 'Look, Doc, I need a photograph of that girl. Suppose you ride out towards Hampton House with me.'

Clancy nodded. 'All right. But how do you get photographs from a mile away?

The logical thing, I should imagine, would be to drive right on up and pay a social call. With me along you can accomplish that. Emily has a little blood-pressure problem. I've been treating it for her for years.' Clancy rose and winked wickedly. 'Would it sound childish if I confessed to a feeling I've always secretly had, that if I hadn't chosen medicine I'd have made a capital undercover man?'

Waltham couldn't restrain the laughter, but Clancy's eyes twinkled; he took no offence. Not even when Peter said, 'Everyone I've ever bumped into has that same feeling.'

They went back to Waltham's car and headed for Hampton House. They used the same secondary road Walter Lee and his companion had used earlier — the same road where Horace Clancy had cornered Pete Waltham.

It was Waltham's first trip up the private road leading to the fieldstone house on top of its small landswell. He told Clancy he thought it was beautiful. Clancy told him that it had once been proposed as an institution for the insane, but that was back before anyone had installed decent central heating, and the board of medical examiners who came like undertakers to look it over, decided that while it had certain virtues as a retreat for mentally disturbed people, it was so damp and clammy eight or nine months out of the year the medical men were sure they'd have round-the-clock work with sufferers from respiratory ailments.

Waltham saw someone come round the side of the house, evidently in response to the sound of his approaching car. Clancy grunted. 'That's Frank, Walter's father. I can tell from here.'

Clancy was right. Frank Lee, dressed as though he might have been doing yard work at the back, greeted them with a wave and a smile. He acknowledged the introduction to Waltham graciously, and in response to Clancy's request about Emily, took them both back round the side of the house to the rear yard, retracing his own earlier steps.

Walter, lounging in tree shade with his

mother and the blue-eyed taffy-blonde Waltham knew would be the radiologist, introduced Waltham to his mother, whom he already knew to smile at in the village, and then to the girl, Janet Bothwell.

She was very attractive. She was also undoubtedly the girl Waltham had seen in the car with Walter Lee; it was the same short, curly, taffy hair, and the girl's shoulders were recognisable.

Clancy said he'd asked Peter to drive him out today because he wanted to see Emily, and also because his own car wasn't functioning too well. None of it was a prevarication. Clancy and Emily Lee went off towards the house together, and as for Clancy's car, it would be perfectly proper to say, at any time, that it did not function properly.

Walter offered a beer but Peter Waltham declined. He did accept the chair Walter's father offered, though, and those four made pleasant conversation for a half hour or until Emily and Doctor Clancy returned.

Frank Lee asked Waltham how he was coming to like their community. The reply was as polite as the query had been. Walter, watching Waltham thoughtfully, then said perhaps Pete would like a few sets of tennis, or some pigeon shooting. There were hundreds of wild pigeons in the woods across the county road, which was estate-land.

Peter smiled a little at the prospect of tennis. He hadn't played since he'd left college a long — wince — time ago.

Walter made the conversation easy. He asked how Peter had made out with his historical research, the last thing he'd heard Waltham was involved with the last time he'd been up.

Peter laughed. 'It wasn't really anything serious. I'm not going to jar Academe with a book on General Washington having secretly kept a harem in Hamilton, or General Arnold having secretly met Major André in your castle, here.'

Walter's father said, 'If you did, believe me, no one would be more surprised than we would. It's a sad but true fact, Mister Waltham, no one ever bothered to write a history of the place. Now, it's impossible. But it would have made interesting reading, eh?'

Waltham nodded. He smiled at the girl. 'Do you like it?' He asked, masking his keen, close interest behind the half-droop of smiling eyelids.

She nodded. 'I think it's fascinating. Especially the tale of secret vaults.'

Walter and his father exchanged an amused look that did not escape Waltham, then the elder man said, 'It would be better if that subject were not brought up before my wife. Once, Walter and some friends of his and I knocked a hole in a wall where one of those rooms was supposed to be concealed. It cost a thousand dollars getting the hole patched up. There was no vault back there, but Walter's mother was furious.'

Janet laughed and Waltham, who had heard the story before, joined in. He had now taken three photographs of the girl with the cigarette-lighter Minox camera concealed in his clasped hands. He had never doubted his ability to do this, providing the sun was right, and since it was afternoon with the brightness coming over his shoulder, and since it had been no accident that he'd taken the chair that would put the sun behind him, the pictures should turn out to be adequate.

Doctor Clancy and Emily returned. Walter, knowing of his mother's ailment, raised his brows at Clancy and got back a reassuring little nod and smile. That was all; no one mentioned blood pressure.

Mrs Lee took a chair next to her husband and said she hoped Peter would visit them often, that when Walter left the house was lonely. She and her husband liked having young people about.

Waltham promised to come again, and as he and Clancy rose to depart. Walter said he'd see them to the car. On the walk back around front he asked Clancy a couple of questions about his mother. Clancy's answers were reassuring, and that topic died. Walter then asked Peter if he intended to be around much longer. It was one of those things that, if a person were already suspicious, could sound meaningful in some sinister context, although it could also be quite innocent.

Waltham shrugged. 'Perhaps another

week or so. Possibly longer because I've become rather fond of the village.'

'Then there's no reason why we can't plan some tennis,' responded Walter. 'Janet likes it and the old courts through the woods behind the house could stand some use.'

Waltham didn't know there were any courts on the estate. They were beside the car when he said, 'That would be very nice.'

'Day after tomorrow, morning?' asked Walter, and Waltham nodded, extended a hand, then climbed into the car. He and Clancy waved as they drove away.

Doctor Clancy looked up rather wryly. 'You *do* play tennis, I presume?'

'I used to,' said Waltham. 'I'll get by. They'll beat me of course, but that only helps relationships. Like being beaten at pinochle.' He grinned and Clancy's eyes twinkled. Then he asked the next, and most obvious question.

'Did you get your photographs?'

Waltham reached for the Minox and handed it to Clancy. He didn't have to reply. Clancy turned the tiny canera over in his hands, then passed it back. He was impressed.

'Sneaky lot, you lads,' was all he said until they were back in the village heading for the hotel. As they turned into the parking area he spoke again, evidently after considerable reflection.

'You really don't think any of those people at Hampton House could be involved, do you?'

As Waltham switched off the car and reached for the door handle he said, 'As I said once before, Doctor, *someone* is.'

'But not those people.'

Waltham stood in the afternoon shadows looking at Clancy. He was satisfied; Clancy was dependable. Whatever he thought of the Lees, or that Bothwell girl, he was not going to go round town shooting off his mouth. Waltham said, 'Doctor, it's one thing to be an undercover man and quite another thing to be a judge. I'm only the former. I seek evidence, put things together so they make some kind of sense. But it's impersonal work with me. At least to the extent that I don't get carried away. You

116

might find that course acceptable, too.'

Clancy's eyes twinkled ironically. 'I do, of course. Except that I've known those people a long time.' He held up a hand to head off the obvious retort. 'Oh, I know how good an actor, or actress, the people you're after have to be.' He dropped the hand and shook his head. 'But not the Lees, lad. Not the Lees.'

They parted then, Clancy heading for home and Waltham entering the hotel to pick up his mail and go upstairs to read it.

There was a rather voluminous report on the people in Hamilton whose names he'd given Washington, and as he knew would be the case, there was nothing in those backgrounds to indicate ideological defection. But then ideology was quite different from nationality. The worst kind of opposition had historically come from ideological enemies. Soldiers wearing different uniforms were never as fierce, nor as cruel, nor as fanatical, when serving the simple cause of nationality, as people who dressed alike, spoke alike, but who thought differently.

Regardless of what the reports turned up, someone in Hamilton was Waltham's ideological enemy. Then he found the last page of that report and read it with a quickening pulse. It did not say Armand Dulette was capable of treason, it simply showed that during the war he'd been a U.S.S.R. prisoner in Poland, later in the Soviet Union itself, and belatedly, after two years, had been repatriated to Canada.

After that the man's behaviour was predictable. He had moved across the boundary into the United States, to Hamilton, Vermont, and had been there ever since, excepting a few trips as far as the U.S. West Coast, and at least one trip to Europe — to France, thence on to Italy, none of which was incriminating in itself, unless Waltham knew who he'd seen over there. And upon that point the report offered nothing except a brief paragraph that said the report in Waltham's hands was only a hastily worked-up and sketchy history of the man; that when a more thorough investigation had been completed it would be forthcoming.

Waltham sat awhile in thought, then re-read each page of the report before putting it to fire, destroying it, after which he wrote a letter back enclosing the roll of film from the Minox, and when he went down to the street for supper, he dropped that letter into a post-box.

He had no intention of waiting for the additional background information on Armand Dulette. He had in mind to either implicate the man or clear him long before that report reached him.

He proposed to start that undertaking as soon as it was dark.

10

First Score!

The electronic listening device called a 'bug' is as easy to install as sticking a bit of coin-sized tape to the underside of a desk, behind a framed picture on a wall, or even affixing it to the underside of a telephone cradle.

Subsequently activating a pocket-sized tape-recorder which is sensitised to receive only the sounds transmitted on the frequency used by the bug, is even easier, because this is normally done some distance from the bug, in more agreeable surroundings.

The trick, and the danger, has always been to put the bug in place. For Waltham, who knew which ground floor door opening off the lobby led to Armand Dulette's suite, and supposed office as well, the chance of getting in during daytime was minimised by old Tom at the lobby-desk, and also by the likelihood of encountering Dulette inside, even if he managed some way to get past old Tom.

At night, after Tom had gone for the day, crossing the lobby unobserved was feasible, but there then loomed large the even greater chance of encountering Dulette in his rooms.

This was of course the real danger, even though Waltham had been schooled to negate it. He was therefore alert and wary as he entered the hotel's dining-room — where he rarely ate — to have his dinner. His reason for eating there this particular night was to make certain Armand Dulette, who always ate there, probably because he owned it, was in his proper place.

He was. They nodded, in fact, as Waltham passed the table, then paused and turned back to bend down and say almost unctuously, 'My apologies for the other night at the tavern.'

Dulette's black eyes appraised Waltham. 'I've done the same things a hundred times, *mon ami*. There is nothing to apologise about.'

Waltham smiled softly. 'That's very generous of you,' he said, drawing back up off the table where he'd leaned. 'They serve powerful drinks in Hamilton.' He went on over to a single table near the street-side window and sat.

Outside, evening was lingering through a time when normally darkness would be all around. That was an indication of the time of year, naturally, but it also helped Waltham see people strolling through the pleasant night, meeting now and then, stopping to converse, or gazing at window displays across the road. The haberdashery, for example, had window-lights illuminating two very elegantly attired dummies. The clothing was excellent, for Boston or New York, or even Washington, but it looked slightly over-done for a place as isolated, as rural and rustic as Hamilton.

Waltham was midway through his meal when Armand Dulette, covering a great yawn, rose and strolled towards the lobby, out of the dining-room. Waltham studied his wristwatch a moment, then went back to eating. He had plenty of time. All night in fact — barring, of course, one of those inexplicable inadvertencies that worried people who were embarked upon things not normally done.

He even sat a moment in the lobby reading the evening paper. Old Tom had departed for the night, as he did every evening, and three or four transient salesmen — at least that was how Waltham catalogued them — stamped upstairs heading for bed, before he folded the paper, laid it aside, went to the front door to scan the sidewalk in both directions, looked again at his watch, then strode swiftly over to Dulette's door, slid an object that resembled an old-fashioned button-hook into the equally old-fashioned keyhole, and opened the door to step quickly inside, into total darkness.

Bachelors, being a queer breed, frequently kept all their window-blinds drawn. This never happened in woman-dominated households, but it applied in Dulette's quarters. Perhaps understandably, however, since Dulette had no frontal exposure, and his rear-wall livingroom windows showed only a back-alley and some picket fences on across that alley.

But that was what made the place so infernally dark.

Waltham could hear Dulette's bubbly and rhythmic breathing through an open door, which doubtless led to the man's bedroom. He expected to hear that; after all, being anything but a novice it had been no difficult undertaking to slip the pill into Dulette's salad while leaning at the table apologising.

The telephone was upon an old, scarred desk near the farthest covered window. Waltham attached the bug, stepped back to examine as much of the room as he could discern in that gloomy darkness, then quietly returned to the door leading back to the lobby.

Men's voices out there turned him motionless. He had no trepidation. Unless those were late-night visitors for Dulette he was in no danger, and even if they were, he was prepared for that too.

But evidently they weren't, for the men finally moved off, and Waltham cracked the door to see one man go trooping up the creaky stairs while the other man left the lobby through the roadway front doorway. He allowed them both plenty of time, them stepped out, used the button-hook-object again, and let out a big breath as he also crossed towards the stairway.

He did not completely relax until he was in the room with the door locked, and even then he had to test the recorder, which was battery-operated and therefore practically untraceable. Not that he expected anyone in Hamilton to know how to trace a recorder plugged into a wall socket, but training and long-habit made him careful.

There was only one detectable sound down there in Dulette's room — wet snoring. Waltham flicked the switch, put the recorder upon the table at bedside, and got ready for bed feeling that he had earned his rest — and his pay — this day, which to some extent made up for the wasted days.

He waited to go downstairs for breakfast until almost nine o'clock, making certain Dulette did not use the telephone. It was an annoying vigil since he was hungry, his stomach growled, and Dulette did not go near his telephone. Finally, at the risk of losing something, he did venture down to the hotel dining-room for breakfast.

Dulette was not there, which may, or may not, have been significant. A few other people were around; in fact, two of those transient salesmen were sharing a nearby table, also having a late meal.

Afterwards, Waltham returned to his room, stood by the roadside window waiting and watching, and when the recorder finally began emanating sounds, they were the clicks of a telephone number being dialled.

Waltham moved back to the nearest chair, sat with the recorder in his hand, and waited. When the automatic placement had completed its additional, but much softer little clicking sounds, a bell rang several times before a man's voice said, 'All right, Armand?' And the answer going back, in Dulette's strong voice, was simply: 'Yes.'

That was the extent of the conversation. Waltham was not surprised, and although he had hoped for at least a little more, he was satisfied.

He now reversed the taped-message, modulated it down so that the gabble of those few words would not be very loud, and when the lull came during which the telephone bell rang, he slowed the tape to a crawl, took pencil and paper from his pocket and, counting out the clicks made by Dulette's dialling, wrote down the number 802-134-99467.

The first three digits, of course, were the nationwide area code for any number in the State of Vermont. The second three numbers designated the part of Vermont where the called number was indigenous, and the last five numerals were the ones assigned to a specific telephone in a specific residence.

He called Washington, gave the numbers, the time of the call, what was said, and asked for an immediate reply. It was promised so he rang off and sat back to wait, letting the little recorder remain in its ON position in the event Dulette would use his telephone again. He didn't use it, but thirty minutes later Waltham's telephone rang. Washington had traced the number to a hotel in Angel Falls, Vermont, a bustling city not far from the Canadian line much favoured by New England honeymooners. Waltham knew the town although he did not recall the hotel. Not that this mattered. The Chief came on the line, evidently having been listening in as the information Waltham had requested had been passed on, and said, 'Pete, don't worry, we'll have a man check that out immediately.'

Waltham said, 'My guess is a Comcarrier being signalled it's all right to move down here and deliver.'

'My guess too,' said the Chief, 'but we have no advance information of one reaching Montreal.'

'Then it could be a Drone from within the States.'

'Possibly. In either event — good luck, Pete. We'll put a tail on him and if it's possible, although I'm not too hopeful, we'll see that you're notified when he's close, and who he is, or at least what he looks like. The usual routine. All right?'

'Yes. I sent in some negatives from the Minox to be developed. Have you received them yet?'

'No, but the morning mail hasn't been distributed yet.'

'The picture of the girl, Chief: Her name is Janet Bothwell. Radiologist at Massachusetts General in Boston.'

'Right. We'll get right on it. Anything else?'

'A man. Armand Dulette.'

The Chief said, 'I liked him for the part too, after boning up on the background. Of course the rest of it's ready. It'll be sent along immediately. Peter . . . ? Mind your Ps and Qs, I think we're approaching some kind of showdown.'

'Anything I should know?'

'Not over the telephone, no. But you'll be briefed. Goodbye.'

Waltham made a face as he put the telephone down. It was always nice to know someone knew something you *didn't* know in this business; that's how people got shot and stabbed, or simply and considerately, bashed over the skull.

The Chief was all heart. No doubt about it.

Someone coming down the corridor towards Waltham's door prompted him to flick the recorder off and drop it between the end of a nearby sofa and the nearest cushion.

Doctor Clancy rapped and growled his name. Pete admitted him, offered a friendly greeting and closed the door as Clancy came in and went as straight as a bee for a chair.

'I've been thinking,' he said to Waltham, and Peter stifled the smile because this too, was part of the undercover-syndrome. 'If those people are meeting in the cellar below this building, Peter, shouldn't it be a relatively simple thing to put some kind of listening device down there and monitor what they are about?'

Waltham nodded. 'Very simple, Doctor. But not worth the risk. If anyone was detected even going into that booth in the alley where the stairs are located, it could blow the whole thing.'

'Well, but don't you want to *know*?'

'Yes. We'll know without taking any more chances than we have to.'

'I see. Dare I ask just *how* you'll know if you don't eavesdrop'

'We're not the only people involved for our side, Doctor. The others are compiling a good deal of scam too. Maybe they're bugging cellars or residences, I suppose they are, but for us, the thing to do is remain as unobtrusive as possible. Okay?'

'Yes, of course,' muttered Clancy, obviously disappointed.

Waltham grinned. 'Doctor; the neatest of all undercover covers is the mask of absolutely innocence; no possible connection. And when you're on top of something like a drop, which is what Hamilton definitely is, the best of all possible ways to blow not only your own cover, but the cover of everyone else connected with the case, even though they may be five thousand miles away, is to let just one person — just one — get suspicious.'

Doctor Clancy didn't argue, but he said, 'I don't see how we wind it up, though. I'm no lawyer by any stretch of the imagination, but I know *one* thing, Peter; if you plan to bring these people to trial, you've got to have sound evidence, and not the circumstantial kind either.'

Waltham didn't even try to explain that bringing the principals to trial did not actually concern him very much. It would have taken too long to explain, and would have revealed too much. For example, there was not a single Comcarrier who couldn't at the drop of a hat produce proof of foreign citizenship, and sometimes even proof of diplomatic immunity, hence a U.S. court trial would very probably result in nothing more serious than prompt deportation.

Another thing was that the National Security Agency rarely let agents appear in court, for understandable reasons, but Doctor Clancy could have made a great argument out of that.

Waltham said, 'Let's go down to the tobacconist's and have a game of pinochle. Now, though, I no longer have to humour you.'

Clancy's eyes sharpened as he rose.

'Humour me? Why of all the conceit . . . I can beat you at pinochle any day of the week.' He strode firmly to the door and wrenched it open for Waltham to precede him down the hallway.

11

A Fresh Comcarrier Arrives

Doctor Clancy proved his boast. He beat Waltham two out of three pinochle games. He might have won the third one too, but his mind kept wandering to that other matter they'd previously discussed, but which he did not bring up in the tobbaconist's shop.

They parted an hour later when a clerk from the general store came rushing in for Doctor Clancy to come at once, someone was having serious cramps. As old Clancy arose he sighed. 'Peter, you wouldn't believe how many appendixes I've carved out. I'll look you up later.'

Waltham returned to his room and sat with the recorder switched on, but Dulette, whether he was in his rooms or not, did not use the telephone.

At two o'clock an agent telephoned from up-state. He made no attempt to identify himself or greet Waltham. He simply gave a car licence-number, the make, year, colour and model of the vehicle, then said, 'Registered in at the Angel Falls hotel as Frederick Hotstetter. Average height, mousy looking, brown hair, brown eyes, slight build, maybe forty. Okay?'

Waltham said it would be enough, since it obviously was all he was going to get, and rang off. He flicked back through his memory to see if the description was close enough to be anyone he knew or had memorised, but it was too general; it could have been any one of several Comcarriers he knew, or it could be a total stranger.

He didn't worry in any case. But it stuck in his mind what the Chief had said about having no prior warning of the man's arrival. That was not impossible, nor even improbable, but it was not common either because the Agency had men covering almost every known Apparatus member in the country.

As Waltham went down to his car this fact was the only thing that really intrigued him. The rest he assumed was going to be routine.

He had dwelt for a short time upon Clancy's suggestion of a bug in the cellar, but then he'd been prepared to do that long before Clancy had thought of it, and the Chief's demurrer had prevented him from going through with it.

But, as he drove northward through town, the thought persisted. It would be very risky, as he'd told Clancy, but beyond the shadow of a doubt it would give him everything he'd need to complete his assignment in Hamilton. Not that he disliked the village; he actually liked it very much, but he was a man who lived on excitement exactly as other men throve on serenity.

Hamilton would be a wonderful place to retire to, someday, but that was still a long way off, and in the meanwhile, he'd like to complete what he'd been sent to do, and move on.

He turned left on to the turnpike for the first time since he'd gone forth to pick up a principal to trail back to Hamilton. The countryside was not very different although in the far distance there were higher hills, actually blue-blurry mountains not too far, in fact, from the international boundary line. Otherwise, though, there were farms and pastures, creeks and forest-fringes, pretty much as existed southward from Hamilton.

He had a fair idea about where he'd pick up this man calling himself Frederick Hostetter. What made it easy to estimate was the distance from Angel Falls to Hamilton. After all, Vermont was one of the smallest states in the entire Federal Union; it was quite possible to cover its full lateral distance without losing any sleep at all.

Waltham parked near an intersection to check his watch, check his binoculars and the large camera he kept in the glove-compartment, which possessed an excellent zoom lens, then resumed driving northward.

It was not very difficult to pick out the correct car when it was approaching head-on, unless the highway had one of those scenic dividers, then it was all but impossible. Fortunately, Vermont had very few such elegant roadways, outside of the major cities, but even so, as long as Waltham knew the make, the colour and style of vehicle he sought, the chance of picking it out of the oncoming traffic was heightened by the fact that traffic was never very heavy in the Hamilton area.

The primary reason he didn't worry about picking up Hostetter's car was the same reason he hadn't worried much about detecting any of the other vehicles; if he missed them on the turnpike he'd still be able to pick them up in the village.

But he kept his score at one-hundred per cent when the Hostetter-car came down towards him. It was travelling at a fair rate of speed and, fortunately for Waltham's purpose, had no other cars nearby.

He made his turn-about a mile farther along, crossed lanes until he was well behind, then cruised along pacing Frederick Hostetter right on down to the outskirts of Hamilton. But this time he changed his tactics. After parking he made no search for Hostetter, but walked briskly around to the back-alley and waited.

Hostetter came through that lavatory window exactly as Waltham had expected, waited a moment to ascertain that no one was in sight, then ducked into the annex to the hotel that looked like an old storehouse, and disappeared.

Waltham strolled back to his own car, took the camera from the glove-compartment and went up to his room with it. He picked out Hostetter's car parked in front of the haberdashery, drew a chair to the window, and waited, zoom-lens properly adjusted.

It was a tedious wait but a rewarding one. When Hostetter came ambling self-confidently across from the hotel towards his car, Waltham took six pictures of the man, two of which caught him close-up and head-on. Waltham smiled, lowered the camera and made a mock bow as Hostetter drove away. Another car promptly sliding into the space Hostetter had just vacated might have gone unnoticed by Waltham, who was beginning to turn away, except that its driver sat over there gazing directly up at Waltham's window.

For a bad moment Waltham stood looking down at that man's lifted face. Then he put aside the camera, stood off to one side of the window and wished he'd also brought up his binoculars. The man's face looked vaguely familiar. If it was someone sent along to watch over Hostetter — some Apparatus individual — then he might very well have spotted a sunlight reflection off the zoom-lens, and now be sitting down there debating what course to pursue.

Waltham had an emergency tactic for that predicament, too, but he shrank from using it even though each passing moment made some kind of action on his part, mandatory.

He got his belt-gun from the dresser, hid it beneath his coat, tucked the zoom-camera safely out of sight, then left the room moving briskly.

In a place no larger than Hamilton it would always be risky, showing a pistol, which was one reason why Waltham shied away from adopting his present course.

The second reason he didn't enjoy what he was about to do was even more basic: What would he do with a captive in a place where he couldn't turn him over to the police without everyone in town knowing about it within an hour or so — including Armand Dulette?

When he reached the sidewalk in front of the hotel the car across the way was empty. He had started to turn when a quiet voice on his left, near the hotel's entrance, said, 'I'm an old friend. Take me by the arm and walk me up to your room.'

Waltham turned. The stranger was smiling at him, a kind of impish, pixie-like smile. Waltham let his breath out slowly. 'Hello, Arty.' He reached to pump the man's hand then pull him towards the doorway. In a soft whisper he said, 'You scairt hell out of me.'

The burly man called Arty kept that whimsical smile as he and Waltham nodded to old Tom at the desk, and started up the stairs. When they were in the upstairs hallway Arty disengaged himself and said, 'I thought I guessed right, the way you got away from that window. Fact is, I was just wondering which was your room.'

Waltham opened the door for the man called Arty to enter first. As he afterwards closed the door he said, 'I knew you'd spotted me, but I thought you were someone from the Apparatus who'd just seen me taking pictures of the Comcarrier who drove out of that parking place a minute ahead.'

'I know. I saw him drive off. Frederick Hostetter from Angel Falls. I've been on his tail all morning. But you're wrong about him being a Comcarrier. He's a U.S. drone; came all the way from Pennsylvania. I've been camping with him for a week.'

'What's it all about?' asked Waltham.

Arty shrugged. 'Who knows?' Then he smiled. 'This is an ideal drop, the little town. It's like something out of an earlier century, what is missing are the horse-drawn wagons.'

Waltham was interested. 'Now that you've delivered Hostetter and he's gone, what is next for you?'

'My orders are to head back to Washington.'

Waltham went to the camera, slipped out the film-magazine and handed it over. 'Hostetter's on six of the exposures. I'll appreciate it if you'll take it along for me.'

Arty pocketed the film, stepped to the window to glance out, then turned and said, 'It didn't take Hostetter long. Do you know where the drop is?'

'Yes, I know.'

'And who the principal is?'

'That too. Are you involved?'

Arty smiled. 'No thanks. I've got a fresh assignment in Florida. If a man's got to go gum-shoeing through life, Florida is the ideal place to do it. Good luck. Don't come downstairs with me.'

Arty left, and Waltham, watching from the window, saw him cross the road, climb into his car and without even a final glance upwards, drive southward out of town.

Waltham had a twinge; it wasn't just Florida, though. He'd been on assignments down there several times. It was the feeling that Arty, not Pete Waltham, was moving on to the next challenge.

He shrugged that mood off, went to shower, and afterwards went sauntering downstairs for a late luncheon. This time when he entered the hotel's dining-room, Armand Dulette was there — in an open-throated sport shirt, coatless and hot looking. He raised a glass of beer in silent salute as Waltham nodded, moving past. Neither of them spoke.

The afternoon got surprisingly hot, considering the fact that the nights were becoming increasingly chilly as August advanced. Waltham returned to his room to see if the recorder would pick up anything, and when it did not he started to believe that Dulette used that private telephone only for his Apparatus business.

That evening he went to one of the other cafés to dine, and encountered Walter Lee and Miss Bothwell. They asked him to join them, which he did.

It was a pleasant meal and a nice meeting. They reminded him he was expected at Hampton House early the following morning and he lied by saying he hadn't forgotten, while as a matter of fact he *had* forgotten all about that date to play tennis.

Walter mentioned Horace Clancy, perhaps because it was obvious Doctor Clancy and Peter Waltham were friends. He said there had never been a physician in Hamilton people thought as highly of; he also said the biggest problem he had was deciding whether to stay down in Boston when he went into practice, very soon now, or whether to return to his home town and become the local G.P.

He smiled at Waltham. 'The money here — just plain isn't, to put it bluntly. In Boston I could make out very well, twenty-five to thirty thousand dollars annually within a couple of years.'

Janet said, 'Which is it, Walt, money or mankind'

Waltham thought that was a fair summary, but when Lee replied, Waltham was less sure. 'Look, love-of-my-life, mankind is a lot more populous around Boston than up here, so if it's a question of doing the most good, then I'd choose Boston.'

Janet shrugged and resuming eating. Waltham said, 'There's no real question then, is there?'

Walter Lee held up one solitary finger. 'One, Pete. One question. Horace Clancy will have to retire within another year or two. Hamilton will then have no practising physician at all. Boston, even without me, will have several thousand.' Lee smiled into Waltham's eyes. 'Now how does it look to you?'

Waltham replied as he rose from the table. 'It looks as though I've got to get home to bed if I'm to trounce you both tomorrow morning. As for the other thing — sleep well, tonight. Doctor.'

They shared a little laugh and Waltham departed.

Outside, there was the beginning of a new moon. It gave no earthly light whatsoever, but the myriad stars did. And there was also a hint of that oncoming chill already even though it wasn't quite nine o'clock yet.

Waltham got to his room, stood a moment looking across Hamilton's rooftops out where yellow patches of window-light showed from the old manor house, and shook his head. What kind of a life does a man really lead when the biggest decisions he has to make revolve around whether to marry a beautiful taffy-haired radiologist and whether to simply wait, and inherit wealth, or whether to work a little harder and earn more of it?

12

Something in the Wind

There were two letters the following morning. The first one Waltham read gave a complete background for one Janet Bothwell. It took exactly two-thirds of one page of legal-size typing paper.

Waltham was not surprised. But then he would not have been surprised if there had been five full pages showing Janet Bothwell as a combination female Jack The Ripper and John Dillinger. People were predictably only one thing — unpredictable.

The second letter wasn't a report at all. It was simply a clipping from some newspaper listing the death of one Thomas Ellingwood. Police thought the murder was a result of Ellingwood supposedly delivering a half million dollars to someone on the West Coast, and the money Ellingwood finally handed over was counterfeit, the other people were arrested as soon as they started spending the money, and police speculated that their apprehension triggered Ellingwood's murder.

Waltham burned that clipping and the letter. He felt nothing one way or the other for Ellingwood. About all he actually remembered was that missing finger on the left hand and the man's size, which had been powerful and massive.

As for how the man came to his end, Waltham wasn't much concerned over that either; somewhere along the line the Chief had made good on his promise. Ellingwood's genuine money had been replaced with counterfeit cash. Very good; it caused not just the elimination of Ellingwood by one of his own Apparatus people, it also furnished an excellent basis for picking up his West Coast people and sending them to prison, and NSA was still above suspicion.

It was, more or less, routine. At least the *results* were routine and that was NSA's primary aim in its work: Get its principals without being involved itself. It worked very differently from the FBI.

Waltham had to go and buy a tennis racket and tennis balls before he drove to Hampton House. He was reluctant because with Hostetter come and gone he felt Dulette might perhaps signal another Apparatus individual, or, if that were not customary, then the Agency might have detected movement somewhere in the direction of Hamilton, in which case they'd want Waltham to know.

Walter Lee was upstairs, Bronson the houseman informed Waltham as the latter stood in the front doorway, but Miss Bothwell was in the sitting-room. Bronson took Waltham on in.

Janet rose to greet him, her smile genuine, her beauty wholesome and refreshing. His reluctance about being there vanished under the onslaught of her smile. He showed her the new racket. She examined it then candidly shook her head, 'I'll tell you a secret, Mister Waltham; I don't know anything about tennis rackets. I only learned to play the game because Walt liked it. My own cup of tea would be a swim in some secluded place on a day as hot as this one is going to be.'

'Yes,' said Waltham, visualising her in a bathing suit. 'I'll agree. But I used to like tennis. That was in college a long while back.'

She squinted up at him. 'That long?'

They laughed as Walter Lee came into the room carrying several tennis rackets and a bag full of what seemed to be tennis balls. He slapped Waltham lightly on the shoulders.

The three of them left the house and walked through a pattern of golden late summer daylight beyond a fringe of trees that lay a hundred or so yards to the rear of the manor house. The tennis court was beyond, out in a mirage-like setting of greensward where more trees on the far side hid it from general view.

The courts were old, perhaps they'd been installed in old Kingsley's time, Walter didn't say and Waltham didn't ask. But the net was fairly new and the grass out here had recently been gone over with a mower. Birds in the trees, annoyed by the intrusion, scolded from their treetop hiding places.

Waltham made a discovery while involved in the first set against Walter: Although ten years had gone by since he'd played much tennis, he was still in good physical shape. He didn't win — he didn't intend to — but he was satisfied that he might have.

They played for two hours, with periods of rest in between, and when the heat finally arrived, they drifted over to a fragrant little bower where some chairs and a metal table stood, sat and relaxed.

It was good companionship, Waltham wouldn't have denied that, but having the instincts of a bird-dog, he felt a little guilty, loafing there with the beautiful girl and the young doctor. His mind kept drifting to other things: To the late, unlamented Thomas Ellingwood, to the old gunpowder magazine beneath the hotel, to Armand Dulette, even to Horace Clancy whom he hadn't seen yet today.

Finally, recovered from the exertion, they drifted back to the house for a bit of luncheon. Waltham tried to beg off, failed, and resigned himself.

The luncheon, served by Bronson and prepared by Mrs Bronson, was beer and a large crab-louis, perfect for the day and the sense of pleasant tiredness that Waltham felt. But an hour later he escaped and drove back to town.

He took a shower in his upstairs room, re-dressed in casual attire and sat for a while with the recorder switched on. No one used the telephone downstairs. His conscience was mildly troublesome; perhaps Dulette had made an earlier call.

Doctor Clancy arrived about three o'clock to report that he had successfully removed the appendix of the person he'd been summoned to look after the day before. He also said he preferred New England winters to New England summers because while he could always manage to get warm, he could not always manage to get cool.

While he was there the Chief called from Washington. Something, he said, was in the wind. Number Three, who had been Six's bodyguard on their previous visit to Hamilton a month earlier, was on his way back, alone.

'It may be the Ellingwood thing,' said the Chief. 'This man is a member of the Apparatus muscle-division. A trouble-shooter. We've studied all the evidence we could come up with, but of course we don't know exactly what instructions he's been given, so we can simply suppose that they are trying to back-track and find out what went wrong. If we are right, Three is very likely going to be after Dulette. It's not possible he'll have any proof that it was your man who exchanged the good money for the counterfeit, but they certainly know that someone, somewhere along the line, did that.'

'Nice,' murmured Waltham.

The Chief's tone changed, became almost airy. 'Nothing in particular to cause you worry, Pete. But keep an eye open.'

'Yes sir.'

Doctor Clancy, who could have deduced very little from the one-sided conversation, showed curiosity when Waltham put aside the telephone. 'Trouble?' he asked.

Waltham smiled at him. 'Always trouble, Doctor. It's the *degrees* of trouble a person gets to look for.'

'I see. And this time . . . ?'

Waltham shrugged. 'They say it's not serious, but I wouldn't want to bet money on that. Tell me something, Doctor; what have you come to believe about Armand Dulette?'

Waltham didn't really care how Clancy answered, he simply wanted to shift the conversation a little to avoid having to answer questions. The best way to do that, always, was to *ask* questions.

Clancy fished for his old bent-stem pipe and fired it up. 'What I *know* about Dulette is what everyone else hereabouts also knows. He's unmarried, was in the Canadian army for a number of years, came down here not long after the war and bought some property — the hotel and that clothing store across from the hotel. Nothing terribly incriminating in that, is there?'

'No. It wouldn't seem so.'

'But what I *think* of Armand Dulette is something quite different.'

'Oh?' murmured Waltham, getting a little interested. 'I'm listening.'

'That clothing store, for instance: The man and wife who previously owned it had a good bit of illness. In fact, the man eventually died. The widow moved away; down to where she had relatives; New York I think it was. But the illness preceding the man's death took all their savings. It was a lingering thing for which no cure exists.'

Waltham's impatience prompted him to say, 'So Dulette bought the widow out.'

'Well, yes. But not quite like that. She wanted to keep the business. After all she and her husband had pioneered it. But the bank would not make the loan.'

'Poor risk?'

Clancy shook his head from side to side. 'No. At that time I was a member of the board of directors. The reason no loan was granted was because the mortgage had been sold to Dulette a year or so earlier, and he'd let it be known that he didn't want any loan made to the widow.'

'I see. But how could he influence you and the others?'

'He didn't influence me. That's when I resigned from the board of directors. The reason he was able to influence the others was because he'd been buying bank stock and had a sizable chunk of it. The other directors, as well as the bank manager, made a choice between the widow and a man who was becoming increasingly influential in town.'

'So . . . ?'

'You can guess the rest; she didn't get the loan, couldn't meet all the obligations that had piled up after her husband's passing — and Dulette gave notice. She didn't make him foreclose, which I'd have done, damn him; she signed a quit-claim deed and got enough cash out of it to buy her one-way ticket to wherever she went — New York, I believe. Does that answer your question concerning my personal regard for Hamilton's latest outstanding merchant?'

Waltham nodded. He hadn't cared, at the outset, but now he found himself liking Dulette even less. He hadn't actually liked the man before, but sometimes it was possible to respect an enemy.

Waltham rose, smiling. 'I've been

trounced at tennis today, so suppose we go down to the tobacconist's and I'll try to reverse that with you at pinochle.'

Clancy was agreeable. But as he hoisted himself up out of the chair he said, 'I'd like to give you a warning, lad. Whatever you can dig up against Dulette, be very careful. He also impresses me as an untidy type.'

Waltham grinned at the designation. 'Does untidy mean violent, Doctor?'

'It's not funny, Peter. Don't forget that Dulette was trained as a soldier for many years. He may be rusty but I would rather think he's not. If he's involved in this other thing as deeply as I think he may be, you'd do well to respect him as your enemy.'

Waltham went to the door but before opening it he said, 'I'll do that, Doctor. You may depend upon it. But if the scam I got over the telephone a while ago is accurate, someone just as — untidy — may be on his way up here to take care of our man.'

He opened the door and held it open. Clancy, on the verge of speaking, looked out into the hallway, closed his mouth and stalked on out. As he passed, Waltham gave him a pat on the back.

Downstairs, the heat was noticeable the moment they stepped out into it. Waltham, almost unconsciously, glanced over at the haberdashery shop where the two elegant dummies in the window smiled back with their fixed features.

Odd that a man supposedly sworn to oppose capitalism on whatever level he encountered it, should use such base capitalistic means for expanding his own little capitalistic domain. But then, Waltham had seen it done before; the most vociferous socialists, when presented with an opportunity to achieve personal wealth, abruptly abandoned all those lofty ideals about helping the toiling masses, and jumped upon the capitalistic band-wagon.

They strolled to the tobacconist's shop with its small bar and, towards the back of the long room, its battered but sturdy old tables, usually patronised by Hamilton's older men, and found one table vacant. Around them other men sat engrossed, some puffing foul pipes, some smoking strong cigars, and a few with cigarettes dangling from their lips. One or two glanced up and nodded, then dropped their heads to concentrate upon their cards again.

A good deal of poker was played here. It was not illegal to play poker, or any other card game, as long as no money changed hands. The chips atop each table allegedly were allotted before a game began, gratis, but Waltham knew better. The games were for cash, chips were bought and paid for in advance, but the stakes were never high, usually averaging a penny for blues, five cents for the reds, and a dime for the white chips. Very rarely did anyone toss a white chip into a pot.

13

A Conversation

The following morning Dulette's telephone rang while Waltham was keeping his vigil. It was an *incoming* call, rather than the outgoing call Waltham expected.

The conversational format was the same; there was no greeting and what was said followed a metaphor supposedly based on mutual knowledge of the topic.

The incoming voice said, 'Too bad about Ellingwood.'

Dulette said: 'I don't understand it. That money came direct.'

'Maybe someone tampered with it at your place.'

'That's impossible. If it was tampered with, it had to happen somewhere else.'

'How do you prove that?'

'Prove it? What are you talking about? I had it safe until it was picked up. No one but I knew where it was, no one at all.'

'Well, I told them you were not that foolish. That you would know at once they would suspect you first of all. Mace is coming.'

'To see me?'

'Yes. I wasn't supposed to say anything. Well . . . you know now, eh?'

That was the entire conversation and when Dulette rang off Waltham played the tape back and listened as closely as before. Mace evidently was the code-name for the muscle-man Waltham knew as Number Three. And the Chief had been right, of course, but he would more than likely be, in any case, since he had all the evidence at his fingertips. More evidence, in fact, than he'd tell Waltham.

There was something else to be considered too. Drops were seldom permanent. Apparatus people, like Agency personnel, moved constantly. It was essential. But Hamilton, which had been such a convenient drop for so long, must be one drop the Apparatus did not cherish losing. Most certainly Dulette, who had seventeen years behind him in this one place, would not be happy about being ordered somewhere else.

After all, dedicated or not, when a person reached middle life a lot of things looked different than they'd looked seventeen years earlier when the lean idealism still mattered.

Waltham put the tape into an envelope and mailed it off, returned to the room and threaded in a fresh tape and sat for a long while just waiting — and thinking.

He could intercept Mace easily enough even though he had nothing very substantial to go on in locating the man before he reached town. And too, there was the element of time. Providing Mace was already on his way from up near the border, as before, Waltham could pretty well guess when he'd arrive.

In the end he decided to do nothing. Not, as he'd implied to Clancy, that he didn't give a tinker's-damn which Apparatus person killed another Apparatus person, although that was actually his basic feeling, but the reason he chose to wait was that although Dulette had been warned, it had not been in any way that implied Mace was actually coming to kill

Dulette. The Apparatus was baffled; someone, somewhere along the line, had replaced the genuine half-million dollars with a counterfeit half-million. But the Apparatus — and Waltham too, for the matter of that — had no idea where the switch had taken place.

That an investigation would start with Dulette was even quite logical. He was the person who initially received the money and handed it over to Ellingwood. His drop, then, was the most reasonable place to start looking.

But if one chose to be pragmatic, then one could go back even farther; to Number Six who had delivered the money.

But evidently, since Ellingwood had been punished, not Number Six, the Apparatus was convinced the genuine half-million had at least reached Hamilton.

Waltham even smiled a little. Dulette was in the hot-seat. It would be interesting to see how — or *if* — he managed to get out of it. Waltham's memory of Number Three led him to feel that Three would not be a very easy person to convince. Unlike Number Six, Waltham remembered the photos of Three he'd studied as showing a fair-complexioned man with pale small eyes, with a slash of a mouth, who stood perhaps five feet and nine or ten inches and weighed a burly two hundred pounds. Mace was in fact a quite poetic name for Number Three.

Waltham hid the recorder and went down to an early dinner. He chose the hotel restaurant because he hoped to see Dulette's face. But Armand was not there and did not appear.

Later, Waltham walked the sidewalks under a night that had none of the usual chill to it. He met Tony Murphy, proprietor of the petrol station he patronised, passed a few words with him, then went along as far as the marquee of the movie-house where he paused to gaze at the scantily clad girls on the posters.

On the stroll back he looked in at the tobacconist's but Doctor Clancy was absent. He hadn't really expected to find him there anyway. Clancy was one of those people who believed in retiring early and getting plenty of rest.

Back at the hotel he saw Dulette engaged in conversation with old Tom at the lobby-desk. He ambled on over wearing a pleasant, amiable expression.

'Beautiful night,' he said, and both men nodded. 'I've been expecting a frost, it's late enough in the year for New England to get one, isn't it?'

Tom replied, while Dulette stood there blank-faced, listening. 'Can come any time after the twentieth of August, Mister Waltham. But many's the year I've seen it go almost until the fifteenth of September before we got more'n a cold snap or two.'

Dulette spoke, finally. 'You're not going to let a little frost run you off, are you, Mister Waltham? You've been a very good tenant. I'd hate to see you leave.'

Waltham shook his head. 'Frost would find me almost anywhere I went. Anyway, I grew up with it. There's nothing to cold weather that plenty of woollens can't cure.'

He had to grudgingly admire Dulette's aplomb. The man stood slouched over the desk as though the only worry he had in the world was Waltham's departure from the hotel.

It was a trifle disappointing. Waltham had hoped to see external signs of the inner turmoil. But of course, dwelling upon it a little suggested that Dulette would never have achieved his position of trust within the Apparatus unless he had icewater for blood and nerves of steel.

'I've been toying with the idea of putting in some ski runs on the slopes north of town,' Dulette said, still looking squarely at Waltham. 'What Hamilton needs is some tourist money. All around us other towns are getting it. Mostly summertime holidaymakers because other towns have lakes or rivers. About all we can try for is the winter trade. What do you think, Mister Waltham?'

'I'm not familiar with the slopes, but if you have adequate ones I think you just might have the germ of a fine idea, Mister Dulette.'

Armand smiled thinly and nodded his head. 'Let's talk more about this over a beer one of these evenings,' he said, and

Waltham took the cue: He was being dismissed.

On the way upstairs to his room he smiled humourlessly to himself. Clancy had been very correct about Dulette; any man as unemotional in the face of a very real threat as Dulette seemed to be, was dangerous.

He expected a signal concerning Number Three but none came. Perhaps it was thought in Washington internal difficulties within the Apparatus were simply something for the National Security Agency to be aware of without getting involved in.

One disadvantage to being in the field rather than at headquarters on the Potomac was that detailed information was not delegated, only general information.

But the following morning, quite early in fact, he got the signal. Mace would arrive in Hamilton before noon. Waltham was to report the moment he picked up anything.

He wanted to protest on the grounds that he hadn't been permitted to bug the old gunpowder magazine beneath the hotel, but fortunately he did not do this. The reason it was fortunate was that the bug on Dulette's telephone transmitted that meeting to him in his upstairs rooms. In other words, Number Three and Armand Dulette met, not in the cellar, but in Dulette's private quarters in the hotel.

Number Three surprised Waltham with his mildness. The bug did not transmit the man's voice with any great degree of fidelity, but the words were enough. Number Three said, 'Armand, no one has accused you of taking the sound money and putting counterfeit cash in its place. What the organisation wants to know is where this could have happened. Not here, but somewhere else — anywhere, you understand — and not because we can't get more money, but because as you'll appreciate, somewhere down the line our cover has been penetrated. *That's* what has scairt hell out of a lot of people.'

'I've thought,' replied Dulette. 'I've been worrying about that money ever since I gave it to Ellingwood.'

'Go on, I'm interested,' murmured Mace in an amiable tone of voice.

'Why does it have to mean the cover's been penetrated? Ellingwood stopped at hotels, didn't he, and he stopped at cafés on his way west. Couldn't he have been knocked over by common everyday crooks?'

Number Three's answer, still soft-spoken, lacked some of its earlier amiability. 'I'm surprised at you. In the first place who would even suspect someone who looked no more affluent than Ellingwood looked, would be carrying a half-million in cash? In the second place, Dulette, what everyday common thieves carry a half-million in phony money around looking for someone to swap with?'

Dulette let out a big, audible sigh. 'All right. It was just a thought.'

'Maybe,' said Number Three, 'such a person might be hanging around here, Dulette. Maybe the cover has been penetrated right here in your quaint little town. Have you considered that?'

Pete Waltham bent closer to the

recorder now, beginning to suspect that Number Three's purpose in being in the village might in fact have more to do with what he'd just suggested than with probing Armand Dulette, or punishing him.

'I told you,' Dulette retorted, a trifle sharply. 'No one knew the money was here. No one touched it except me, between delivery and Ellingwood's arrival. Listen; even you couldn't have found it, Mace.'

'Armand,' the other man said, dropping his voice to that soft tone of amiability again. 'What's so secret about the cellar? Anyone can blunder into that annexe out back and go down the stairs. Don't come at me about the door being kept locked. A kid could wrench it open. And everyone knows about that old cellar down there. Just the fact that you have told them it's falling in, that it's dangerous to go down there isn't going to keep any snoopy kids or even any . . . '

'The money, Mace, was not in the damned cellar!'

Dulette said that so sharply that for a

moment Number Three said nothing. He may have resented the sharpness in fact although Waltham, breathlessly intent on the recorder, had no way of knowing that.

Finally, Number Three said, 'All right; it was out yonder then. Armand, if you found the passageway . . . ? See what I'm getting at?'

'Oh, of course I see. But I'll take you downstairs right now and bet you a thousand dollars you can't find it. Are you game?'

Again Number Three gave a delayed answer. 'All right. But I don't have any thousand dollars to wager.'

That ended the conversation. Waltham sat waiting for something more but only silence came in on the feedback. He then removed the tape, sealed it, wrote a short, brusque note to go with it, dropped both into an envelope and went downstairs to post the letter in the kerbside mailbox.

After that he returned to the room, threaded in another tape and sat for a solid hour waiting for Dulette and Number Three to return to the room downstairs, but they did not return. In fact, they did not return to that room together at all. Waltham sat waiting, impatience and frustration making his nerves crawl. They did not come back.

Later in the evening when Waltham chose to dine in the hotel restaurant, neither man was present. He had his first grave doubt about Dulette's safety despite the fact that Number Three hadn't sounded antagonistic in that earlier conversation.

How long would it take a professional muscle-man to turn antagonistic? An hour, thirty minutes, five minutes, ten seconds?

14

The Cellar

Waltham kept his vigil the next day too, but except for what he took to be doors opening and closing, a man's heavy footsteps down in Dulette's room, there was nothing to be recorded.

He took an hour off to stroll around town searching for Number Three, but never found him. It occurred to him that perhaps Three had completed his investigation and had departed.

Perhaps it wouldn't have taken any longer to make that investigation than a couple of hours, an overnight delay, perhaps, at the most.

Waltham wasn't really too concerned, except that he wanted to know where Number Three was. Something, as the Chief had said, was happening, and at least in the Hamilton area Peter Waltham was smack-dab in the middle of it. There were better places to be from the standpoint of personal well-being and feelings of security. Dulette he felt he could keep in sight without much difficulty, but with Dulette *and* Number Three the odds were piling up a bit more than he liked.

Finally, there were the enigmatic things that had been said in the Dulette-Mace conversation. For example, what passageway had Dulette and Mace referred to, and when Mace had said, 'out yonder' what had that meant?

Waltham returned to his room to resume his vigil with the recorder although he did not expect anything, and as a matter of fact he did not hear anything.

At seven o'clock that evening he got a signal from the Chief. The tapes had arrived but only a brief mention was made of the first one. It was the tape he'd mailed that morning by airmail that the Chief was interested in.

'There are a couple of things I don't understand, Pete, and I think when we unravel them we'll have about what we want. The first one is — what did Three mean by 'out yonder'?'

Waltham took the telephone to the window where a little breeze was coming in cooling things off. He leaned there as he spoke, looking out over the village rooftops towards the manor house. 'I have no answer for you on that,' he answered. 'Nor to that remark about a passageway, but with your permission I'll bug the cellar and that ought to — .'

'All right, bug it. We have about all we need anyway. The cellar is the rendezvous-spot and this Armand Dulette is the principal. Fine.'

'Chief, I got the impression from that second tape that Hamilton as a drop may be slated for extinction.'

'What of it?'

'Dulette has lived here seventeen years. He's the town capitalist.'

'He wouldn't like that description.'

'He's a middle-aged man, Chief. I just don't see him folding his tent in the night and going somewhere else to start over again.'

'He'd better, if he's ordered to.

Anyway, that's not our kettle of fish, Pete. Incidentally, I'll send up another man if you'd like. Is Three still around?'

'I don't know. I haven't seen him, and there've been no further talks in Dulette's rooms.'

'Do you want another man?'

It was a temptation, but Waltham finally said, 'No. I'll call if that changes. Anything further?'

'Report the moment you've finished bugging the cellar. I want to know you've made it successfully. Otherwise — well — we'll be interested. Goodbye.'

Waltham grimaced at the telephone after he'd put it aside. The Chief wasn't subtle. He'd never been subtle as a matter of fact. But if he thought Waltham was going to be caught bugging an ancient gunpowder magazine he was mistaken.

Nightfall seemed to be coming a little earlier the past few days, or possibly it was his imagination. While he waited for full darkness he slid the gun-holster onto his trouser-belt, then clipped in the snub-nosed magnum revolver. It was a small weapon, and light in the hand, but a

.350 magnum bullet ploughed a hole through human flesh like a lightning bolt would also do.

He returned to the window to savour that little breeze. Now, he could see those cheery orange windows out at Hampton House. He started to turn away. It was now dark enough to visit the basement.

Something hit down hard in his mind, freezing him where he stood for a second, and afterwards causing him to gradually turn back and stare out the window.

Passageway . . . direct line from hotel to haberdashery across the street . . . direct line from haberdashery out to old manor house . . . where there was supposed to be a legendary secret room . . . A half mile of underground passage-way would connect all three! *Out yonder.*

'Damn,' he breathed softly, and leaned for a moment upon the windowsill making an estimate of the length any such passageway would have to be. Finally, he turned, got out the tape recorder and spoke into it putting on tape this seemingly wild idea. That was in case anything *did* happen, and others would have to come to Hamilton and clean up after him.

After that he put this idea out of his mind and concentrated only on what lay ahead. Number Three had said a schoolboy could force an entrance to that rustic old annexe out behind the hotel. Waltham hoped this was true, not because he wasn't adequately equipped, and trained, for picking locks, but because that was the most vulnerable place for him to be seen.

He left his room, turned right along the hallway instead of his usual left-turn, and descended to the lower floor by a servant's stairway, unlighted and narrow as well as being musty-smelling.

He came forth into what appeared to be an old bathroom although the tub, if one had actually ever been there, was gone, with just two capped-off water pipes protruding from a flaky papered wall.

Beyond this room he found a small hallway that led off at a northerly angle towards lights. From the smell, that room on ahead had to be the kitchen. He waited in darkness for a long time to make certain there was no one close by, then he glided past the lighted doorway and came to a thick old oak door leading out into the yonder alleyway.

It took an agonisingly long time to get the rusty old door-lock to respond. There were people working in the kitchen, he could hear their voices now and then.

The door eventually yielded and he stepped through out under a star-splashed sky with a few familiar sounds coming down to him in the sooty alleyway. A dog was furiously barking over on the other street, westward, and someone closer was playing either a radio or a record player too loud.

The little shed where he'd hidden once was not very far distant on his right. To his left and directly along the rear wall of the hotel was that jutting little after-thought of an annexe. He headed directly for it the moment he was satisfied he was quite alone.

The danger of accidental discovery haunted him as he bent to look at the door-lock. It was one of those simple, oldtime latches with a keyhole-shaped orifice. Waltham dug out the buttonhook-object, inserted it gently and caught hold of the only roller to such a lock, pulled it easily back, and twisted the knob as he pulled. The door opened soundlessly.

It was as dark as the original pit the moment he closed the door after himself, and although he had a pencil-torch in a pocket he did not use it.

For a moment he stood silent, just listening, but when no sound came from down the stairs or from outside, he began groping his way along.

The air was dank and stale. Twice he' encountered cloying cobwebs and paused to tear them free. Annoyance made him wonder why a spider would build a web in a place where insects would not voluntarily appear because of the infernal darkness.

The stairs, remarkably enough, were as solid as though the wood was new. He guessed that it *was* new wood. They were also rather steep, doubtless erected over the excavation the original builder had made.

By count there were twenty-four of them. After that the stale smell increased and he was standing upon hard earth. Now, he used the pencil-torch to examine the old cellar.

There were no crumbling walls. In fact, the walls were of stone and mortar without a single crack anywhere. Waltham guessed these old walls would be several feet thick, but without any way to test this, nor any desire to do so right then either, he satisfied himself with making a very careful study of each wall independently and separately.

What he sought, of course, was some opening that would support his hunch about the passageway leading out to the manor house. But if there *was* any such opening it was not in any of those four walls.

He wanted to look further but he'd already been in the cellar several more minutes than he should have been, so he picked a likely place to plant the listening device — under the hoary lip of a rough, embedded stone — made certain by using the torch the bug was adequately hidden, then turned towards the stairs while putting up the little torch.

A faint rustling sound froze him where he stood. It came from up the stairway where it was darkest. His first fear was that someone was trying to enter from the alleyway but since the door was not locked and no one ultimately appeared, he decided it had to be some kind of rodent, possibly a rat, perhaps as startled by the scent of Waltham as Waltham had been startled by the sound of the rodent.

He started on up, the stairs did not squeak, and when he reached the top landing and halted to listen close to the door, that little rustling sound came again, but now it was farther away, somewhere down below in the cellar behind him.

As before he waited, then reached for the door, twisted the knob very softly, pulled, and when he could see stars he stepped through and fished out his hooked implement to lock the door after himself.

He did not re-enter the hotel by the door he'd used earlier to leave it, but made his way along the alley northward to the first intersecting street, and there, finally, stepped forth into plain sight, striding towards Main Street.

He didn't fully relax until, passing the tobacconist's dark establishment, he was confident there was no one behind him. Then he stopped, looking in at the window display of pipes, tobacco, and cigars, and let his muscles loosen.

The darkness of that stygian place hadn't been the worst part, nor had the little rattling toenails of the rat; what he had liked least was being cornered down there with only one way out. If anyone had caught him in the cellar from the stairway he'd have had no way to escape at all.

Resuming his way, he strolled to the front doorway of the hotel, glanced in before he quite got to the doorway, and got a shock. Armand Dulette was standing with his back to the street over by the lobby-desk, which was empty now, old Tom having gone off duty some time earlier, talking quietly to Number Three.

Not being completely recovered from

his recent adventure, Waltham turned, stepped off the kerbing and crossed to the front of the haberdashery where he examined the window display while letting the surprise of finding that Number Three was still around, wear off.

It took a moment or two for this to happen because he finally knew just how lucky — there was no other word for it — he'd been, in that musty old cellar.

With the odds still two-to-one, if he'd been caught down there by Three, he would undoubtedly still be down there — on his back — by now.

It might not have been a close call at all, but he chose to view it as such, and he also chose to continue his walk up as far as the nearest corner where he crossed the street one more time, and started back down towards the hotel.

Dulette and Number Three were gone. He paused at the roadway window to look in, ascertaining this, before entering the lobby himself.

He guessed they were in Dulette's rooms but felt no motivation to make certain of that, so he climbed the stairs, and almost to the minute, entered his own room one hour since he'd left it.

He got the recorder, switched it on and listened. There wasn't a sound to be detected from either listening device. Almost with relief, Waltham put the recorder on his bedside table and got ready to retire.

It had been, in some respects, a rather dull day, but he couldn't have said that was also true of the evening!

15

Another Clue

Waltham called Washington in the morning to say the listening device had been safely planted in the cellar. In return, he was informed that a Comcarrier was arriving in Montreal that very morning, that the man's cover-name was Hoffman, and that a tail would escort him over the international boundary line but would not, being one of Canada's internal policeman, go any further with Hoffmann. The Agency, confident where Hoffmann was going, confident too that a word to Waltham would take care of Hoffmann quite adequately, reported that there was no intention to have an Agency man tail Hoffmann from the line to Hamilton.

Waltham was given the usual particulars, only in this case it was a purely personal description. He was certain he'd be able to pick the man out. It was on the tip of his tongue to mention that with Number Three still in Hamilton, with Dulette on hand, and now with a third Apparatus agent arriving, things might be getting somewhat out of hand. The reason he did not mention this was because of something he was told.

'There's been a shake-up in New York and another one out on the West Coast as a result of that counterfeit money. It wasn't planned this way, but it's certainly working out favourably. They know their cover has been penetrated somewhere, and it is beginning to appear that everything is being frozen until the leak has been discovered In other words, at your end, the assumption here in Washington is that this fresh courier is simply going to pass the word to Dulette to lie low. You can verify this for us if you detect any of their conversation.'

In other words it was beginning to appear that Dulette and Number Three were not going to be engrossed in anything other than this threat to the Apparatus, which should make them relatively harmless at least for the time being.

Waltham went down to breakfast in the hotel dining-room and although he was on time for the meal along with a dozen or so others, Armand Dulette was not present. Whatever that signified it at least made him think that Dulette did indeed have something on his mind. As for the man called Mace, Waltham did not see him either.

After breakfast Waltham drove to the local museum and again studied that old floor plan of Hampton House. He guessed which of the alleged secret rooms the Lees had searched for without finding. It was not hard to divine that the vault behind the fireplace was not the one they'd torn out the wall looking for because he'd seen that fireplace and it had shown no signs whatever of having been disturbed.

He spent most of the morning looking over other old maps of the village, reading a number of old journals, and even got interested in the gunpowder statistics, but found no other reference to secret rooms, or tunnels.

It did not deter him but it *did* make him wonder why it was, if some such underground passageway existed, and had been built at some expense and labour, there was no mention of it.

Of course, back during the Rebellion it would have been a secret, but over the ensuing centuries surely someone would have recognised the quaintness of such an undertaking and would have mentioned it.

He got the curator, an elderly woman, in a general conversation which ultimately got round to the gun-powder magazine beneath the hotel. She was very helpful, but she was also unable to shed any light on further local excavations, except to say that north of Hamilton there had once been a log fort, built before the Rebellion to withstand redskin assaults, and out there one could still discern the sunken outlines of several cellars and trenches.

On the way back from the museum Waltham speculated on who, if anyone, might have heard legends of an old passageway. There were still a number of the original families around. In the end, though, he let it drop. Short of making an issue of it, which would inevitably arouse curiosity — and talk — he would have to rely upon his own initiative.

But he was certain there *was* some such passageway. He could imagine any number of reasons for it to exist; so that the poor-grade gunpowder manufactured in Hamilton could be smuggled out of town, perhaps, or in order that clandestine militia organisations could come and go. If he could have found out more about Hampton House's original developer he was sure he could have then had something to either substantiate or fault his theory of this passageway running out as far as the manor house.

It was as he was parking his car in the area beside the hotel that an idea crossed his mind. If that passageway ran beneath the haberdashery store as he'd theorized it might, then there would be some kind of entrance to it over across the street.

A cheery feminine voice scattered his thoughts. 'Hello there. You look like someone with a lot on his mind for so lovely a day, Mister Waltham.'

It was Janet Bothwell, dressed in a pale yellow frock that set off her golden-tan skin and taffy hair to perfection. He smiled. 'I was plotting a devious strategy to beat your fiancé at tennis.'

She laughed. 'I wish someone would. He's too good at it.' She turned, looking across the street. 'He's over there buying some shirts at the clothing store, then we're going to lunch down the street. Why don't you join us?'

'Three can be a crowd,' he murmured.

She shook her head and sunshine glinted like clear water in her curly hair. 'He'd be agreeably surprised. He likes you. As for me — collecting handsome men could become a hobby of mine.'

An idea came to Waltham. 'Let's go over and check with him. The last thing I want to do is intrude.' He didn't give her much chance for additional conversation, but hooked his arm through hers and started across the street. He'd never been inside the haberdashery and this was a golden opportunity to look around. Not that he expected to see any holes in the floor or any musty old narrow doorways, but if he could get some idea of the lay of the land over there when he returned in the night — which he firmly intended to do — he'd at least know what to avoid and what to seek.

When they entered the store he saw Walter Lee and an elderly, rather bird-like man, at a counter where the older man, evidently the store's sole clerk, was wrapping several sports shirts. The older man glanced up and gave Janet a warm smile, and Waltham a more perfunctory smile.

Janet told Walter her idea and he smilingly concurred. 'Just let me get squared away here,' he said, holding a packet of money in one hand, 'then we'll go eat.'

Waltham had a moment to look, which was what he'd wanted in the first place. The store had a rear room, partially visible through a doorless opening beyond the counter. Otherwise it had wall-racks for sweaters, suits, shirts, socks, the general inventory of a clothing store, and there were two recessed mirrors, three slanted ones to each little alcove so that viewers could see themselves from different angles.

There were several tables in the centre of the room piled with additional clothing, and near the rear of the room was the show department. The overall appearance was of a well-stocked, successful business establishment, obviously too, the store had been in its present location a long time. That would have been obvious even if Waltham hadn't learned it from Doctor Clancy.

Walter came forward with his purchases, grinning. Ready for another set-to on the tennis court?' he asked Waltham, and when the reply took the form of a grimace, Walter laughed. 'The least I can do by way of appeasement is buy your lunch.'

But they went first to Walter's car where he left the bundles, then, with Janet between them, Walter struck out for the hotel dining-room. Waltham would have preferred dining elsewhere, for no particular reason actually, though, so he trooped along in smiling silence.

This time he saw Dulette. The man was evidently just finishing his midday meal. He seemed in something of a hurry, too. He looked twice at his wrist as he gulped down the last of his tea and rose. Walter nodded and Dulette, glancing up, saw the three of them and nodded back. His gaze lingered no longer on Waltham than it lingered on the other two.

They took a table near the roadway window where filtered sunshine came through, ordered, then Walter sighed and, glancing briefly out the window, said, 'Two more days then I'm due back in Boston.' His head swung back. 'I envy you, Pete; loafing around here as though you hadn't a worry in the world.'

It could have been spoken as the result of private curiosity, or it could have simply been a frank statement of fact. Waltham passed it off as the latter by saying, 'I've earned a long holiday. But I'll have to say it's been more pleasant than I expected.'

When their meal came Janet studied Waltham over the rim of a tea cup. 'You impress me as a professional man.' She smiled artlessly. 'That's being nosy, isn't it?'

'I couldn't take offence even if I wanted to. You're far too pretty. As a matter of fact I did take a degree in law.'

She nodded, judgement vindicated. 'I'll remember that if I ever decide to sue someone.'

Waltham didn't pursue it. He had a degree in law but he had never taken a State Examination anywhere and therefore was ineligible to practise law. He'd gone directly from law school into the National Security Agency.

'That store,' he said to Walter, 'has as good an assortment as one could find in the big cities.'

Lee nodded, chewed briefly then said, 'The odd part about it is that Armand Dulette, that glowering individual who owns this hotel where you're staying, also owns the place. Odd because if I ever saw a sloppy dresser, or a man not built for patrician dress, it's got to be Dulette.'

'But a nose for a profit is more important, isn't it?' asked Waltham gently.

Lee nodded. 'Exactly.' He then told

Waltham the same story about Dulette's acquisition of the haberdashery that Doctor Clancy had told him. Only Walter Lee concluded by saying, 'It didn't work out quite as happily as Dulette anticipated, though. The second year after he'd got hold of the property the floor began to give way. It cost him some money shoring it up again.' At Waltham's steady stare, Walter shrugged. 'It's an old building. Almost all the buildings around here are; people have been shoring them up or replacing old timbers, or adding wings and roofs ever since I can remember.'

Waltham wanted to ask who Dulette had employed to repair the floor, but Doctor Clancy came ambling over from the dining-room doorway, puffing happily on his pipe.

They made room for him at the table although he declined to eat, having, or so he said, eaten only an hour or so earlier. He looked at Waltham. ''Was hunting for you. I'm ready to take you on at pinochle again.'

Waltham smiled. 'He beats me every

time. It must be some kind of crutch for his ego.'

A half hour later they parted outside the hotel, Walter and Janet heading across the street towards his car, Waltham and old Clancy turning to slowly stroll in the direction of the tobacconist's shop, although neither seemed very anxious to get down there and start their game.

Waltham said, 'Who did Dulette hire to fix the floor in the haberdashery shop a couple of years after he acquired the building?'

Doctor Clancy looked up. 'Two outsiders. Why?'

Waltham groaned softly. He should have known Dulette would bring in Apparatus men for that job.

'Why?' repeated Clancy. 'Do you think there's something under that floor?'

They reached the tobacconist's doorway and turned in. Waltham did not reply to the question until they had their table in the rear of the room. 'I don't know, Doctor. Maybe there is, it's just a guess. Tell me about the clerk.'

'Old Clarence at the haberdashery

store? He's been clerking there for ten years or so, is harmless, lives with an older sister on the south edge of town. Descendent of one of the old families. Thoroughly harmless and a nice enough chap. You don't suspect *him too*, do you?'

Waltham could only offer the same answer. 'I don't know. Possibly not. Let's get on with the game.'

Clancy kept studying his companion but he asked no more questions. Patently, he hadn't stopped being curious though.

Waltham didn't play a very good game. He was memorizing the layout of the store, and when he'd got that fixed in his mind, he recollected Dulette's seeming anxiety at the hotel dining-room. To Waltham that simply meant that the Comcarrier called Hoffmann was due, and of course *that* meant that instead of sitting there playing pinochle, Waltham should be upstairs in his room at the hotel with the recorder turned on.

16

An Offer Declined

Later, having been beaten three times in a row at pinochle by Horace Clancy, Waltham got away only by promising to show up later for dinner down at Clancy's house. He'd never been there, at least he'd never been *inside* the house, before, and was mildly curious. Clancy assured him that the housekeeper would prepare their dinner as though Clancy thought that might have accounted for Waltham's hesitancy when he accepted.

But that hadn't been what had bothered Waltham at all. He wanted to be left alone in his hotel room with the recorder this evening. He could perhaps have explained that to Clancy but he didn't. Being habitually close-mouthed was not something one overcame on the spur of the moment.

But he had most of the afternoon and

part of the early evening. It was his opinion that if anything was to be done between Hoffmann and Dulette it might be accomplished during that time.

It was a good guess. He'd been sitting in his room a long hour when an incoming telephone call was monitored by the recorder. Someone who didn't bother to identify himself beyond saying he was calling from Philadelphia, asked if Hoffmann had arrived. Dulette tersely replied that Hoffmann was there in the room with him. The person in Philadelphia then asked to speak to Hoffmann, and the ensuing conversation between those two was cryptic but interesting. The person in Philadelphia said: 'Send Mace to Omaha. He's to meet Camel there.'

The voice Waltham assumed belonged to Hoffmann answered briskly. 'It will be done. Has something turned up in Omaha, then?'

'Something,' admitted the other voice. 'Goodbye.'

Hoffmann replacing the telephone made Waltham wince. The instrument beneath the cradle was very sensitive.

Then Hoffmann addressed Armand Dulette. 'Omaha. They think they've picked up something out there on the counterfeit money. Mace is to go to Omaha at once.' Hoffmann's voice seemed to brighten. 'What a relief. I've always said the worst part of this business is not knowing. One minute you are walking along minding your own business, the next minute they are all around you closing in.'

If Dulette was pleased about the Omaha development, he didn't sound much like it. He said, 'Well, after you've been involved as long as I have you'll stop looking over your shoulder.'

'Yes of course,' replied Hoffmann, slightly sarcastic now. 'How long did they say you'd been here? Seventeen years?'

'It could still happen, my friend,' growled Dulette. 'But I don't think about it.'

Hoffmann seemed to tire of this exchange, because next he said, 'It should be a relief to get Mace off your back.'

Dulette manifested that same mood of displeasure again. 'It will be a relief to get you *both* off my back. After all, this drop has only managed to function so well for so long because no one who visits me here, stays on. Hamilton is one of those places where, if a stranger lingers, questions are asked. The secret of our success here has been based on people arriving in the morning and leaving the same morning.'

'You lack subtlety,' muttered Hoffmann. 'Anyway, I suppose the telephone call means there will be normal resumption.'

Dulette remained sullen. 'If so, then I'll be informed. In any case you've done your duty, eh?'

'I'll leave first thing in the morning.'

'Why not tonight?'

Hoffmann swore. 'Damnation! I was on a lousy plane all night, and getting down here all day. What do you think I am, some kind of machine? Now show me where I sleep!'

Dulette muttered something the listening device did not pick up, which was the end of that conversation. It had been enough, though, Waltham immediately deposited both the tape and the usual little note giving location, time and date, in an envelope and went downstairs to post the letter, air-mail. With any luck the information should reach Washington by morning.

He returned to his room, showered, changed, and sat a while longer waiting for something else to come up. Nothing did, however, so he looked through his luggage for additional tapes, discovered that there were only three left, and tried to guess whether that would be sufficient or not.

Then, as the sun sank, he stood to one side of the roadway window and made a long and careful study of the front of the haberdashery store across the street. Later, with dusk settling in, he left the hotel and took a brisk little healthy walk around the opposite square.

The back of the haberdashery building opened upon a cluttered little narrow access alleyway, evidently not often used if one were to judge from the mounds of old crates back there, nearly closing the alley in several places.

The rear door of the building was

metal-covered, as though some local fire ordinance had been enforced once. The lock, however, appeared not to be used, for above it, bolted through, was a heavy hasp from which dangled a sturdy detachable lock. Since these were on the outside of the door it was fair to assume that the last thing the clerk did at night after leaving the store, was lock that door from outside, then pursue his way on homeward up the alley.

It wouldn't be difficult to ascertain if this were in fact the case; simply wait around and see. But Waltham couldn't do that this particular night, and he was not a man inclined towards patience under the circumstances. He didn't want to have to wait another whole day just to make sure when, and how, Dulette's hireling locked up and left.

On the stroll northward to Doctor Clancy's residence he made a mental inventory of the things in his pockets. He had come prepared to enter the store tonight. It was his intention to use the dinner at Clancy's place to fill in the time between now, and when it was late enough to run the risks of breaking and entering.

There was a moon, and except for a few very distant puffy clouds the sky was clear and bright. He would have preferred more darkness, but on balance it seemed that the night would be co-operative. Hamilton retired early, the local constable habitually did the same, and if neither Dulette or his aged clerk suspected anything there would be little reason to be apprehensive.

Clancy was waiting in his old-fashioned, warmly snug and littered parlour when Waltham arrived. Clancy at once pressed upon him a mug of mulled ale. Waltham was reluctant; New England ale, like New England cider, had the kick of a healthy mule to it.

The dining-room table was set, a grey, buxom woman moved back and forth from kitchen to dining-room, and almost before Doctor Clancy and Waltham had been permitted to half finish their drink, and converse a little, she came to say in a no-nonsense tone of voice that dinner was served.

It was one of those typically no-nonsense New England meals, too. Mounded, creamy mashed potatoes, roast beef with dark, tart gravy, fresh bread and butter. The coffee was served black and strong, and the salad was one of those moulded things in which gelatine was used to bind everything together.

Waltham watched Doctor Clancy put away food with great gusto and wondered privately if the old gentleman had ever read any of those ominous articles that constantly appeared in the nation's newspaper and magazines about the perils of excessive caloric intake.

Clancy caught one of those glances and guessed at once what was behind it. He winked. 'The trick, my boy, is not to live forever, but rather to live while you are alive.'

'Is that what you tell overweight patients?' asked Waltham.

'Depends,' grunted Clancy, 'on the degree of excess weight. Now, in my case, I simply estimate how much heavier I am than I should be, add to that the fact that my mother and father both lived into their nineties — not unusual in New England — then I arrive at the figure which is fair for my own longevity.'

Waltham smiled. 'And?'

'Well, I am five feet and nine inches tall, and weigh a shade over one hundred and seventy pounds. I am sixty-four years old, and should, by my calculations survive until about my seventy-fifth year. If I dieted and was careful about crossing the street, I might possibly get through to eighty. But it would be a pretty tasteless and juiceless existence, and in any event, I'd die, wouldn't I?'

Waltham laughed. 'Good enough. I'll accept that, and pending the working out of my own destiny, would you please pass those potatoes?'

Doctor Clancy passed the bowl then said, 'It would be more difficult to estimate your longevity. For example, your interest in the haberdashery might — I said *might* — entail some inclination to have a private look about in there.'

Waltham kept right on eating. It was a close guess, but that was all it was.

'And as ready as I am to agree that our

local constable is hardly any Wyatt Earp, on the other hand, there is Mister Dulette, a distinctly untidy person.'

Waltham raised his eyes. 'Suppose I told you, Doctor, that the stastistic for people falling off tractors on farms and the statistic for people killed in the Vietnam War, on our side at least, showed that more people were hurt on farms?'

'I would reply, my boy, that talking about statistics and *being one*, are very different.'

'The constable goes to bed early, Doctor.'

'True. But does Dulette?'

Waltham nodded. 'Score for you.'

Clancy's pale eyes glowed. 'Then I was right, you do intend to break in.'

'Tonight, right after I leave here.'

Clancy digested that in silence, reached over for his coffee cup and sipped in thought. After a while, finished eating, he groped through his pockets for his pipe, stuffed it with shag and lit up. Finally he said, 'Well, if your mind is made up, of course . . . I could go and pay Dulette a visit for an hour or so.'

'High blood pressure, Doctor?'

'No. Diabetic.'

'You're joking.'

'My dear young man, don't show your ignorance like this; a robust physique does not guarantee much more than a robust heritage. I've seen thousands of people in my lifetime who looked the epitome of health, and who had all manner of internal ailments.' Clancy glanced at his wrist. 'It'd seem a bit late for a call, though,' he mused, and studied Waltham again. 'You couldn't be persuaded to wait until tomorrow night?'

'I'm rigged out for tonight.'

'I see. Whatever that means.'

The housekeeper swept in from the kitchen to remove their plates and afterwards bring two large bowls of strawberry shortcake topped with mounded whipped cream. At Waltham's rueful expression old Doctor Clancy laughed.

'You don't have to eat it.'

'It's a particular weakness of mine,' said Waltham, and dug in.

After a while Clancy said, 'On second thoughts, Dulette just might think it odd if I showed up for a visit this time of night. So I'll simply keep lookout for you.'

Waltham almost shuddered. 'You stay here, smoke your pipe, count your calories, and keep entirely out of it. I don't really need a helper. But I'm grateful that you offered.'

That was the way it ended, but Doctor Clancy protested again, out on the front porch as Waltham was leaving. 'I don't like it, lad. Anyway, what will you find — besides perhaps a cracked skull?'

Waltham made a concession to his training. 'If you're really that interested I'll come back here afterwards and tell you what I've found.'

'I'll wait up, then. Come round back. I'll have all the lights off in the front of the house. No point in advertising, is there?'

As he walked back up through town after thanking Clancy for the splendid meal, Waltham smiled broadly in the darkness. That part about dousing the lights in the front of the house was delightful; there never was as good a secret agent as the one who really wasn't. At least in the field of imagination, anyway.

17

Saved!

It was almost too easy.

The littered back-alley had two feline occupants when Waltham walked up it to the rear of the haberdashery, one of whom fled so precipitously he upset a large cardboard box, which in turn sent the other cat in headlong flight also, but not until he and Waltham had exchanged a curious stare.

The padlock responded to a needle-pointed pick and even the door, when opened, made no sound. Of course a particular disadvantage to picking an outside padlock was that it could not afterwards be closed, and anyone passing by would notice that it was hanging loose. In this case that danger was minimal. It would be unusual for someone to be alley-strolling after ten o'clock in the village of Hamilton.

But the easy part was over for Peter Waltham. He had the lay of the place in mind and had no difficulty avoiding tables, counters and chairs, but although he searched very diligently in the cluttered back-room, he found neither a trapdoor in the floor nor a wall-door. In fact, barring the metal-wrapped alley-door through which he'd entered, there was no opening in the back-room at all, or if there was one, he didn't find it.

The larger room out front, where everything was displayed, seemed an unlikely place for a secret opening, but he searched, aided somewhat by the reflected moonlight coming in past those grinning dummies in the front window.

It was not for want of experience at this sort of thing that he failed either; he'd not only been schooled, but practical experience too, took him to every place one could reasonably expect to find some form of access to what lay below.

He had one unexplored avenue which he kept for the last: The basement, whose slanting doorways outside in the alley had seemed just too obvious. But with only the streetside display window and its slightly raised footing left, he was beginning to assume that the basement would have to provide the entrance. It also crossed his mind that there just might not be one after all. Perhaps, when Dulette'd had the floor shored up, he'd sealed off any access that might have previously existed.

But then, why would Dulette have wanted the store? As a simple business investment? Waltham pushed those thoughts out of his mind, bent to examine the raised flooring of the window display area, and a car cruising past made him drop flat as reflected headlight brightness bounced off the walls.

His left hand encountered a small brass rung set in what looked exactly like a wall electrical outlet. He explored it a moment while remaining prone, then, resisting an urge to use the pencil-torch, pushed his face closer as he caught hold of an edge of the rung, worked it up, slipped two fingers through and pulled.

The floor covering, a worn shag-rug, interfered until he pushed it away and pulled again. The back of the raised dais where the dummies stood gave a quarter of an inch and one of those dressed figurines wobbled. Waltham caught his breath and lunged with his free hand to grasp a plastic ankle. The dummy had been teetering towards the large window.

For several seconds Waltham simply clung to the dummy holding his breath. Then he rose up slightly to consider the predicament. Obviously, the dummy was standing on top of a portion of the floor that could be raised. It may have been an accident, and then again it may not have been, but in either case, since the show-window faced the street, if Waltham moved that dummy anyone at the hotel who happened to glance over would see only one figurine where always before there had been two. But he was too relieved over grabbing the figure's leg before it toppled, breaking the window and making a great racket, to worry much about being forced to give his presence away by moving the dummy.

After a moment he got up very slowly, lifted the dummy to one side, then bent to ascertain the extent of the width of that hinged opening. The only possible way to lift that segment of raised platform enough to lower himself down through it, would be to remove the dummy.

For a moment he regretted not accepting Doctor Clancy's offer of assistance, but only for a moment. He was this far and had no intention of being frightened off, even though Armand Dulette could very easily ascertain by glancing at the store-window, that all was not right within. It was a chance. He'd taken bigger ones. Finally, after ascertaining there was no wire connected to the dummy, he raised the platform and shone his tiny torch into the rank blackness below.

There was a steel ladder rather like the ones found bolted to the sides of buildings for emergency or fire use, dowelled to one stone-and-mortar wall. That would be the access. But farther down his little light showed nothing more than a cellar.

He eased over, grasped the ladder with one hand, let the platform down over his head very gently with the other hand, and was immediately plunged into a limbo of blackness so dense he couldn't see his hand in front of his face.

The little torch helped as he descended, but even it was limited in its penetration, so deep was the darkness. When he reached the cellar floor a cold breeze that smelled of dampness came steadily towards him. It was a good omen. Using the torch he started walking.

For the first fifty feet the tunnel had adequate height, but after that he had to bend forward, and even then he occasionally bumped something overhead. But what he thought might lie ahead — damp earth — was not encountered.

The walls, ceiling and floor of this subterranean place had been painstakingly mortared with fieldstone. It was the same variety of New England granite Hampton House was constructed of. And although this tunnel was very old — not to mention unhealthy — it did not appear to have suffered much over the centuries from Vermont's frightful winters.

Waltham went along until he was quite

satisfied he had to have passed far beyond the limits of the haberdashery store up above, that littered alley behind it, and even those streets and residences that were upon the adjoining avenue above. He turned back, finally, feeling triumphant, and also beginning to feel the chill of that ceaseless cold air that seemed to emanate far ahead.

Success did not mean anything more than that he'd found his tunnel and had proved his theory correct. Until he could make a more detailed exploration there was no way of knowing whether, in fact, the old tunnel actually went out as far as the manor house.

He thought that it probably had, once, but whether it still did or not remained to be proven. By the time he got back to the ladder his fingers were stiff from cold. He put away the little torch and began his hand-over-hand ascent, being careful to make no sound. At the last step he hung there listening for any sounds inside the store. There were none. At least he could detect none, so he raised the floor to the window-display and climbed out.

It had to be at least twenty degrees warmer above ground than it was beneath it, down in that tunnel. He replaced the clothes dummy exactly as he'd found it, smoothed out every vestige of his visit and turned to go back through the rear room and out.

Two blurring shapes moving almost simultaneously made Waltham whirl and crouch. In the fraction of a second he had before being struck, he recognised the shadows as human shapes. Then one of them fell powerfully against him. He lashed out, hard, buried a fist to the wrist in a yielding stomach, and fell with the unknown man on top of him.

A voice hissed in suppressed excitement from farther back. 'Get from under him! Smartly now, lad.'

Doctor Clancy! As Waltham shook loose the limp form and got upright the older man leaned for a closer look.

'He's knocked out,' he whispered, voice shaking.

'Why did you follow me?' whispered Waltham.

Clancy raised his face in the gloom.

'Lucky thing for you I did.' He thrust what seemed to be a fence-slat towards the sprawling man on the floor. 'He was just creeping in through the back door when I came along and spotted him. I found this stick in the rubbish at the back. We both saw you coming out of the floor at the same time. Only I wasn't sure it was you. Then he got ready to lunge, so I hit him from behind over the head.'

Waltham dropped to one knee. 'The damned dummy,' he muttered, and Clancy, evidently believing Waltham was referring to the unconscious man, said, 'Leave him. Let's get out of here.'

Waltham looked up shaking his head. 'We *can't* leave him. Give me a hand up with him.'

'What the devil for?'

'Doctor, you bought in, so now you take orders. Lend a hand!'

There was neither the time to explain nor to argue, so Clancy helped hoist the limp figure across Waltham's shoulder, then they slipped out into the dark alleyway and started hurrying northward. Clancy knew all the back ways for getting to his residence unobserved, but by the time they got there Waltham's legs were about to buckle. The man on his back was not only dead weight, he also happened to be very heavy.

In Clancy's pantry they could turn on a light. Waltham, breathing hard and looking rumpled, said, 'Number Three.'

Doctor Clancy seemed not to have heard as he bent over the unconscious man examining the gash on the back of the man's head. Evidently satisfied, he afterwards straightened up. 'He'll make it. He'll have a headache for a day or so, but at that he's lucky. I can't recall ever doing that before, and perhaps I was leaning a bit much when I clouted him. Thick skull, thank goodness. Now then — who is he?'

'A man they call Mace, an Apparatus investigator, which is a polite name for a muscle-man.'

'A killer?'

'Possibly. Where can we leave him, Doctor?'

Clancy was aghast. 'Leave him? Do you mean here in my house?'

'Or in a shed or a basement; perhaps your garage.'

Clancy seemed to swallow hard. He dropped his eyes to the prisoner again, made a grimace and said, 'Why not drive him out of town somewhere and leave him? He'll be all right.'

'Look, Doctor, he knows someone has found the tunnel.'

'Found the what?'

Waltham swore in exasperation. 'I told you I'd come back and explain, and I'll do it, but right now get me some tape before he comes round and starts yelling his bloody head off.'

Clancy left the pantry and in his absence Waltham took everything, including a short-barrelled revolver with a screw-on silencer, out of Mace's pockets. There wasn't anything very incriminating except the weapon and its appurtenance, but anywhere in the United States that appurtenance would have caused Mace a lot of trouble. Guns were not always illegal to possess, even to carry, but silencers very definitely were.

Clancy returned and handed over the

big roll of tape. As Waltham knelt down to tape Number Three's hands behind his back, and to silence him effectively with more tape, Clancy said, 'We can put him in the woodshed out behind the garage. No one ever goes out there. But how long will he have to remain there?'

'Only until I get someone up here to haul him away,' replied Waltham, finishing his work with the tape. 'Now help me lift him up again.'

Clancy led the way. They put their prisoner on some old quilts and sacks in the rather airy shed, and Clancy afterwards stoked up his pipe with shaking hands as he said, 'I don't think I'd be such a good undercover man after all. I never cared much for violence.'

Waltham grinned downward. 'You acquitted yourself very well for a non-violent person, Doctor. Now suppose we return to the house. I've got to call Washington and arrange for Mister Mace to be carted away.'

Clancy led the way back, puffing up little clouds of fragrant smoke as he hiked along. Inside, he set about making a pot of coffee after showing Waltham where the telephone was.

The night-officer at NSA headquarters in Washington was not the least ruffled when Waltham, still somewhat breathless, related what had happened and what he wanted done. A team would be up the following day from the Boston office to take Number Three away.

Waltham relaxed for the first time since dinner, thought a moment of the havoc he'd barely got out from under, then rose and went tiredly back to the kitchen for a much-needed cup of coffee, all thought of his triumph forgotten for the time being.

18

A Night of Surprises

Doctor Clancy was astonished to learn there actually was a tunnel beneath town. At least beneath a part of it. He had, he said, made quite a study of the village some years back as a sort of after-hours hobby, which of course accounted for his familiarity when they visited the museum and other places, but he had never read anywhere that a tunnel existed.

He was interested in knowing how Dulette, who was not a native either, and who had less interest in the area's historic past, had found out where the tunnel was.

'When the floor to the haberdashery sagged,' said Waltham. 'Maybe he knew before, but after that happened he most certainly knew.'

'But it seems so unlikely,' protested Clancy, 'that over all those years someone didn't leave a note about the tunnel, or a plan, or write of it in a diary or journal.'

'Possibly they did and others destroyed it. Or possibly the men who built that tunnel weren't local men. Tell me, Doctor, were soldiers billeted here from other parts of the country?'

'Certainly they were. And there was a prisoner stockade out where that old log fort stood'

Waltham smiled. 'There is a possible answer. Captive redcoats may have made the tunnel under the supervision of their captors. They sailed back to Britain when the war ended.'

Clancy nodded. 'Well, however it got there, it's surely a fact at any rate. But what's it being used for now?'

'I have no idea,' confessed Waltham, re-filling his cup from the pot on the stove. 'What I'm concerned about is the gentleman in the woodshed, and Armand Dulette. He still has a visitor named Hoffmann with him. If they haven't already discovered that Mace has disappeared they very soon will.'

'Do you know this man's car? We could hide that too.'

226

'Not good enough, Doctor. Mace's personal effects would still be at the hotel where he was staying. No man would jump in his car and drive away from a town without taking his razor and toothbrush, and so forth.'

Clancy was convinced. 'What, then?' he asked.

Waltham was thinking of that and *had* been thinking of it for some time now. Hamilton as a drop was finished, he was certain of that.

The Apparatus was always wary. Total changes were oftentimes made when someone simply breathed a suspicion. A thing such as had occurred at Hamilton would bring an order for everyone to scatter, change names, change identities, lie low for several months at the very least.

It was, actually, a rather awkward situation. Waltham's orders had not been to break up anything, merely to ascertain who the principal was, in Hamilton, and where the meetings were held.

He had done that. He had also done a little more. Perhaps the chief would feel the event leading up to blowing everyone's cover by clouting Number Three was part of what he'd been sent north to do. Again, the Chief might feel Waltham got a little zealous.

That was how he felt about it, personally. He'd got carried away.

'Well,' Clancy said, tapping the table-top, 'you'd better come back from wherever your imagination is taking you, because before too long it'll be dawn. We are going to need some kind of plan.'

'Can't make one until the team arrives from Washington to take our prisoner away.'

'Speaking of him, he ought to be coming round by now. Perhaps we ought to go and have a look.'

Waltham shrugged. There were a number of things Mace could tell him, but he had very little hope that Mace ever would. Apparatus people were frequently quite fanatical, even self-sacrificing.

They took a cup of black coffee with them, Doctor Clancy's suggestion. It was chilly in the yard out back, and very silent. Apart from the street lamps there didn't seem to be a light shining anywhere in the village.

Mace was conscious. He had done what he could towards keeping warm by burrowing into the sacks and old quilts. He looked hard at both his visitors but looked longest at Waltham.

Clancy bent to lay a hand lightly upon the boundman's head. He then worked loose the tape over Mace's lips, but shook a finger as he stepped back.

'Don't raise your voice, Mister Mace. Otherwise we'll tape you up again. Care for some hot coffee?'

Clancy had to help Mace drink because they left his arms bound behind his back. The coffee worked wonders. Mace's bleary eyes still reflected pain, a headache, but his attitude changed a little. He said, 'All I remember was going into the store.'

Clancy was obliging. He told what had happened. Throughout this recitation Mace's gaze went to Waltham and remained fixed there. Finally, Mace said, 'Mind telling me who you are, mister?'

Waltham nodded. 'I mind. But you tell

me about the tunnel and I'll tell you who I am.'

Mace didn't even blink. 'What tunnel?' he asked, and Waltham had to admire the man's poise.

'The tunnel beneath the haberdashery store, Mace. The tunnel Dulette uses. It also goes beneath the hotel — but you'd know about that, wouldn't you'

Mace listened carefully, drank more coffee when Clancy helped him with it, then he said, 'Someone sure was blind, weren't they? And there you sat, right there in Armand's hotel. Mister, you're an Agency man, aren't you?'

'Tell me about the tunnel,' said Waltham.

Mace forced a smile with pain in it. 'Tell you nothing, mister.'

'How about Hoffmann; is he a dedicated person too? Or maybe by now Dulette's a little disillusioned. Seventeen years making a nice comfortable niche in a drowsy little pleasant village could soften a man.'

'You're wasting your breath,' said Mace. 'And you've played hell by kidnapping me, too.'

Clancy interrupted to say, 'It's cold out here. Give me a hand, Peter; we may as well take him into the kitchen.'

'What about your housekeeper, Doc?'

'Well — I'll telephone a bit later and give her the day off.'

Mace could walk along between them, and seemed eager to do so. Inside, he looked around, found a kitchen chair to his liking and sat. It was blessedly warm in the kitchen.

Clancy got a pain-killer from his office at the front of the house, gave it Mace with a second cup of coffee, and when Mace seemed revived enough to ask them to free his arms, Clancy pronounced him nearly totally recovered from his 'accident', but they did not free his arms.

A car driving slowly out front diverted Waltham. He went through the darkened front of the house to a window. The car crept gently to the kerbing out front and stopped.

Waltham wondered. He was reasonably certain he and Clancy hadn't been seen returning with Mace from the store,

231

although that was really one of those things he couldn't be positive of. If they hadn't then that wasn't Dulette out there in the car. If they *had* been seen . . .

Two men alighted, one on each side of the car. They met on the pavement out front and paused to look around. Neither of them was Armand Dulette, for aside from acting like strangers, neither of them had Dulette's physique.

If they were Agency men from Boston they must have been driving all night. Waltham unbuttoned his coat, stepped to the door and eased it open a crack. The two men were coming up Doctor Clancy's steps. One of them said, 'If this isn't it we're going to have an irate citizen on our hands.'

Waltham relaxed and pulled back the door. 'Arty,' he said, startling the newcomers. They came inside, let Waltham close the door, then the beefier of the two, a tallish man, shoved out his hand. 'Peterson,' he said. 'You're Pete Waltham.'

As Waltham dropped Peterson's hand he asked if the duo had driven all night They nodded. 'Chief sounded pretty insistent. He said you have one of their muscle-men.'

Waltham turned and beckoned, leading them out to the kitchen where he introduced Doctor Clancy — and Mace. The newcomers studied the prisoner impassively and silently. Their attitudes seemed to bode no good for Mace.

Clancy offered coffee and Arty accepted. Peterson stepped over to examine the revolver with the silencer that was lying upon a sink. He turned and said, 'Were you supposed to hit Dulette?'

Mace gave Arty look for look and did not so much as open his mouth. Waltham shrugged. Mace had been fairly talkative before the newcomers had arrived. Peterson, putting the gun aside, turned and smiled slightly at the prisoner. 'You've got a long ride ahead of you, friend. All the way to Boston.'

Mace spat a word out. 'Kidnapping!'

Peterson fished forth a folded paper from an inside coat pocket. 'Not quite. This is a federal warrant for your arrest.'

'What charge?'

'Illegal entry.'

Mace squeezed out a bleak laugh. 'Kind of late getting around to it, aren't you? I've been in the U.S. fifteen years.'

'No, it's not late,' replied Peterson, pocketing the folded paper. 'We wanted you free, Comrade. You've been like a seeing-eye dog for us.'

Mace glared. 'Go to hell. Your day is coming. The lot of you.'

Peterson then said something that stopped Waltham's breath for two seconds. 'By the way, we think you were on the right track about the phony money. Where we traded cash with Ellingwood isn't where the *real* exchange occurred, Mace. You see, *we got counterfeit money too.*'

Mace and Waltham simply stared their incredulity. Arty shrugged as he saw Waltham's expression. 'It's a fact. That idea we had to making the swap was fine. There was just one thing wrong — someone had beaten us to it.'

Waltham felt like saying 'Are you sure?' but of course that wasn't necessary. Any time the Agency said it had got hold of counterfeit money, there could be no doubt of it at all.

Mace spoke next. He was still staring at Arty. 'Correct me if I'm wrong. What you're saying is that someone inside our organisation gave Ellingwood phoney money before you people penetrated us and made your own switch. Is that right?'

Arty nodded. 'Right as rain.'

'And,' began Mace, but Arty shook his head. 'This isn't a social gathering. You'll have your chance to talk in Boston.'

Mace wasn't quite ready to let go, though. 'What you said about me being on the right track . . . '

Arty lit a cigarette. 'You know what I meant.'

Mace sat perfectly still a moment, then said, very softly, 'Here? Right here in Hamilton?'

'You can do better than that, Mace. You can name him. We already know who he is anyway.'

'Dulette . . . ?'

Arty nodded. 'Armand Dulette.'

Mace reacted. 'I don't believe it. It's just not so. You've cooked this up for — .'

'Save the air,' said Peterson, stepping

up behind Mace, catching hold and heaving the burly man to his feet. 'We've got to be out of here before sunup and you're gabbling like a parrot.'

Mace tried to hold back but Peterson had a surprisingly deceptive strength. At the door leading towards the dark front of the house Mace turned one last time. 'Waltham; get him. By gawd get Dulette!'

Peterson gave a hard shove, sent Mace stumbling into the next room and Arty smiled at both Waltham and Doctor Clancy. 'I don't know how much time you've got here; I would imagine that if this one got on to you Dulette and anyone else around shouldn't be far off. Whatever you've got to do, Pete, I'd try and do it before noon. Or perhaps ten o'clock.'

Waltham nodded. He'd already reached these conclusions. But there was something else. 'Wait a minute, Arty. I'll walk to the car with you.' He nodded towards Clancy. 'Excuse me a minute, Doc. This won't take long.'

Clancy nodded silently and stepped to the stove as though prepared to either heat up what coffee remained, or to make a fresh pot. Off in the east beyond the kitchen window there was a cold kind of hushed greyness spreading outward from a sooty horizon.

The new day was dawning.

19

The Final Exploration

When Waltham returned a little later Doctor Clancy's coffee pot was cheerily perking and the aroma was pleasantly filling the warm kitchen. Clancy yawned and sat at the kitchen table as Waltham took a chair across from him. Clearly, Clancy was expecting an explanation.

Waltham didn't hold back this time. Clancy had proven himself a dependable ally. Outside, the greyness was firming up, turning a very soft pale blue over where earth and sky mingled in the distance.

First, Waltham explained about the money, how it had been switched and the reason. 'So Ellingwood would inadvertently cause serious trouble for the Apparatus on the West Coast.'

Clancy looked a trifle caustic as he said, 'What happened to Mister Ellingwood?'

'Dead,' replied Waltham, and frowned at Clancy. 'Doctor, this isn't a game of marbles. Those people take care of mistakes, even innocent ones, very effectively. That's how they play the game.'

'And you?'

'The same way — with their people — when we have to. Now let's get back to our own problem.'

'Which is simply that Armand Dulette has stolen some money.'

'Not just *some* *money*. A half million dollars.'

Clancy pursed his lips and rose to amble over and get the coffee pot. He refilled their cups in silence, put aside the pot and resumed his sitting position before finally speaking. 'Well, he wasn't as dedicated as he should have been, was he?'

Waltham's cynicism came out. 'I've never seen one that was *that* dedicated, Doctor. A half million dollars is an awful lot of wealth.'

'But they were close, and they'd have killed him if they'd found out, wouldn't they?'

'No doubt of it. You heard the last thing Mace said to me as he left this room. Get Dulette. But knowing the man, I'd say he would take that kind of a chance. I'd even say he's probably been a gambler for big stakes most of his life. That's what a professional soldier has to be, isn't it?'

'I suppose so. But now what'

'I want the money.'

Clancy looked up. 'You?'

'Not personally, Doctor. I want the money as evidence, and I also want Dulette.'

'I would somehow rather imagine you'll have some trouble getting either one.'

Waltham gulped his coffee, sat a moment thinking, then arose as he said, 'I'm going after Dulette now. He'll be the key to the money.'

Clancy didn't argue. 'All right. What do you want me to do?'

Waltham looked steadily at the older man, and Clancy returned his stare. Obviously, if Waltham told Clancy not to get involved, it wouldn't work now any better than it had worked earlier. 'Wait one hour, then rout the constable out of bed and take him to the alley behind the haberdashery store. When that clerk shows up, have the constable arrest him.'

'You surely can't believe old Clarence knew anything about all this?' protested Clancy. 'The man's the very soul of rectitude.'

'That soul of rectitude,' replied Waltham sarcastically, 'couldn't have worked all these years in that damned store, making the window displays, without knowing about that trapdoor, Doctor. How *much* he knew, I won't take the time to guess right now, but I don't want him or anyone else behind me if I have to go back down into the tunnel again.'

'That's all you want me to do?'

'You can show the tunnel to the constable, and tell him to keep out of it until he talks to me. You can also look for a man called Hoffmann who may still be around. He's another Apparatus man.'

'Arrest him too?'

Waltham nodded, glanced at his wrist and straightened up. 'Good luck, Doctor.'

Clancy didn't smile as he replied to that. 'I'm not the one who's going to need the luck. If you need me I'll be around the store.'

Waltham left. Outside, dawn was breaking. A noisy old truck, inward bound, perhaps from some local farm, went clattering past with what looked like aluminium milk tins in the back. The driver threw Waltham a cheery wave, perhaps mistaking him for Doctor Clancy in the poor light. Waltham waved back as he strode down towards the hotel's lonely lighted lobby, which was empty when he reached it, the time being a bit early for old Tom to be on duty.

It was cold, even in the lobby, while outside where pale stars lingered in an even paler sky, it looked as though it just might be a cold day. The season was sufficiently advanced for cold days to begin.

Waltham crossed the deserted lobby to Dulette's door, and hesitated a moment debating whether to knock or to pick the lock. In the end he chose to use the button-hook-object. There was always the possibility that an alerted or suspicious Armand Dulette might open the door gun in hand.

But the moment Waltham eased back the door and stepped inside he had a feeling that if he'd knocked he wouldn't have got any response. The place had that feeling of being empty, sensitive people could detect.

The bedroom showed that although someone had indeed slept in the bed, they hadn't been there for some time now. The sheets were cold to the touch.

Dulette's clothing was not draped on any of the chairs and a large rug, one of those New England hand-woven circular floor coverings, had been kicked to one side. Waltham switched on a bedside lamp because, as elsewhere throughout Dulette's quarters, shades kept down at all times prevented much visibility, even in broad daylight, which it wasn't yet in any event.

The trapdoor was there before Waltham's eyes. He stood a moment studying it, and finally it dawned on him why he'd found no exit from the cellar below which would lead into the tunnel. The cellar was farther back; perhaps twenty or thirty feet eastward of the area directly beneath the bedroom. It probably at one time had been connected to the tunnel, but someone — probably Dulette himself — had seen to it that there no longer was any connection. In this way he could use the cellar for his clandestine meetings without any of his visitors even suspecting there was a tunnel.

He reflected that seventeen years had given Dulette all the time needed to manifest each secret facet of his character, and something that had been said back in Doctor Clancy's kitchen seemed true; Dulette's greed out-weighed his idealism, which did not completely surprise Peter Waltham; as he'd said back there, or at least had *thought*, this had happened many times before.

He switched off the bedside lamp — no point in advertising his presence should Dulette be waiting down there, armed, which he most certainly would be, exactly as Waltham also was.

It didn't seem very probable that Dulette would still be below. That cold bed indicated that he'd been gone some little time. If he was down there at all it was a fair guess that he was much farther along; perhaps even at the terminus — wherever that was — with his stolen wealth.

It crossed Waltham's mind, as he stepped lightly over and hoisted the trapdoor, that Dulette might even have Hoffmann down there with him, although this seemed very unlikely. A man who had got away with stealing a half million dollars would be unlikely to take in a partner *after* he'd committed the theft. Particularly another Apparatus man.

There was an identical steel ladder leading downward, perhaps made by the same person, and installed at the same time, as the one across the street in the haberdashery store. Also, it was just as pitch-black below the bedroom as it had been below the store.

Waltham loosened his jacket for easy gun-access, but after standing perfectly still for a bit, just listening, he felt confident that no one was close by. In fact, he didn't hear anything at all until he took several steps, then the soft echo of his own footfalls rose up round him in the tomb-like darkness.

He reluctantly shed his shoes and walked on without them. The stones weren't sharp, too many feet had passed across them for that, but they *were* damp and cold.

Now, making no noise at all, and with the pencil-torch in his left hand, which left his right hand free for emergencies, he started forward. That chilly breeze brushed his cheeks.

He paused beneath the haberdashery store to shine his thin blade of light up at the steel ladder he'd used earlier. After that, partly because he wasn't all that familiar with what lay beyond, either above or below, he began to lose his sense of distance and location. Not that it mattered very much; the tunnel went arrow-straight, had no other outlets, and once committed, a person could only go either forward or backward. He went forward.

His feet got cold and after a while, when he had to stoop a little to avoid bumps, it seemed that time had stopped, that distance had increased, that he was in a world of unending night walking a rough treadmill.

Once, something made a tiny rattling sound up ahead. Waltham stopped in his tracks, his feet seeming very vulnerable to rats, or whatever it was that had made that frantic little rattling sound.

He gave the other tunnel-occupant all the time needed to get away, then he started forward again, more careful now, and from time to time, when he dared, shining the light around. The last thing he wished to do was accidentally step on a rat and be bitten.

The cold breeze seemed to be coming a little more strongly as he moved along, as though, whatever its source, he was getting closer to it.

He was fairly certain that by now he had left the village behind and was moving along beneath that handsome greensward that surrounded Hampton House. He also estimated that his depth underground had to be at least eight feet, and perhaps more, for otherwise, surely when the road that passed the Lee estate had been constructed the excavators would have found the tunnel.

He did *not* dwell on what would happen if Dulette, up ahead somewhere, heard him coming and prepared an ambush. There was no way at all to avoid injury in the tunnel if Dulette opened fire; even dropping prone wouldn't do much more than perhaps delay the inevitable. The tunnel was less than six feet high and no more than four feet wide, and it was straight. A reasonably tall, broad man it this place was literally a sitting duck.

But being barefoot helped him avoid making noise. Also, he felt his way along with his extended right hand. There was no hurry in any case. If Dulette was up ahead, unless he knew another way to return to the village unseen, he'd have to come back the same way he'd got up there, and providing he suspected nothing, the advantage might lie with Peter Waltham.

The greatest peril was that Dulette would be using a torch. But Waltham only passingly reflected upon that as the chilly little breeze became steadily stronger, only now it seemed to have a faint scent of wood-ash to it, or fireplace embers.

Waltham stopped, pocketed his little torch and made a guess. That breeze was coming down the chimney of the manor house's great living-room fireplace! Otherwise, how account for the scent of ash or embers? That being so, then Frank and Walter Lee were wrong; there *was* a secret vault in their mansion, behind the fireplace, exactly as it was shown in the old floor-plan at the village museum.

Going a bit farther, that would be where the tunnel terminated — where Dulette now was, and without much doubt, was also where he'd cached his stolen half million dollars.

Being right, or at least feeling fairly confident he was right, didn't make Peter Waltham feel like bursting forth into song, for he was evidently approaching the climax of his stocking-footed stroll, and on ahead was something infinitely more deadly than a startled rat. Armand Dulette, the Apparatus man who had spent quite a few years of his life being, as

Clancy had put it, 'untidy'.

He held his wrist inches from his face and noted the time as being shortly past eight o'clock in the morning. He'd neglected timing himself in the tunnel, which would have given a fair idea of the length of the thing. But that didn't matter right at the moment either.

He started on ahead with the fragrance of wood-ash getting noticeably stronger. Up above, very likely, the Lee family — and their house guest Janet Bothwell — were probably beginning to stir if they were late risers, or possibly were having a pleasant breakfast, while beneath their feet, gopher-like, their friend Peter Waltham was silently gliding along in a world of soundless night.

20

Capture!

When the smell of ashes was strongest Waltham stopped to assess his surroundings. As far as the tunnel was concerned nothing had changed, but now it was possible to discern a difference in the air. It was less stale and seemed a bit warmer. He felt the ceiling above, found it warm to the touch, and speculated that he was either directly beneath the fireplace hearth or was very close to it, perhaps midway beneath the large living-room of the manor house. Probably, a fire being kept burning most of the year, heat was able to penetrate this far down underground.

He went forward another ten feet and saw the first sliver of light. It lay above, and outlining, one of those steel fireplace ladders.

Journey's end!

He felt his weapon, which was reassuring, in fact, which was the *only* reassuring thing at hand, and inched closer to get a better glimpse of what was ahead and above.

The ladder and the opening above could have been back at the haberdashery store, or beneath Dulette's bedroom, it was similar in every detail. Even the hollowed place, although smoother to the touch as though this were much older stone, had the same funnel-like appearance.

As for the light, obviously someone up there had not bothered replacing the rug or whatever was normally used to hide the trapdoor from above. On the other hand, for Waltham to climb up and raise that trapdoor would be to invite a bullet in the forehead.

He climbed the ladder very gingerly, testing each rung and each hand-hold before easing on up with his entire weight. Finally, head bent sideways to avoid brushing the trapdoor's underside-braces, he detected faint voices, masculine he thought, and not very close.

Having no idea where he was in relation to the rooms of the house, he was driven to assume that the room above was large, perhaps as large as the living-room or the formal dining-room, and that the talking men were somewhere off a bit.

He considered lifting the trapdoor a crack but hesitated until he'd felt for the hinges, ran his hand over both of them to see if there was oil. There was, which meant that Dulette — or someone — didn't want this door to squeak, either. But the voices began to sound slightly louder, meaning the men above were coming back. Waltham controlled an instinctive feeling of panic. If someone up there threw back the trapdoor, there he'd be, hanging to the ladder fully exposed. He felt for the belt-gun and gripped it although he did not draw it. Not yet.

It was impossible to make out what was being said. The voices were low, deep, and muffled by the trapdoor, but there were two of them, Waltham knew that much, as they began fading again, as though the people possessing them were moving off again.

Now, when he could barely hear them, Waltham took his chance, eased the trapdoor up a fraction of an inch at a time using his shoulder as the lever, and when light poured past down into the tunnel below he could see above the floor-level.

The room wasn't large at all. In fact, it was some kind of narrow, elongated corridor. Possibly some passageway between two of the house's mighty exterior walls.

A naked bulb hanging from twisted wires accounted for all that brightness. There was a battered old table and two chairs at the far end of the room, and the trapdoor was close to them, near the northernmost extremity of the place.

He saw Dulette, at least he saw the back of a man he was sure had to be Armand Dulette, facing away from the trapdoor and talking earnestly to a second man Waltham could not make out because Dulette's shadow obscured him, and also because there were other shadows over there.

There was no sign of any money but there was the outline of two valises against a wall, reflected there from on top of the nearby old table.

Dulette's argument seemed to grow in vehemence as the smaller man, attired in lighter clothing, held out. Dulette waved his arms and raised his voice, which finally seemed to impress his companion because the other man very distinctly said, 'All right. But it's a hell of a way to end up. What we are doing is selling out. Treason, or whatever you want to call it.'

Dulette growled something and waved his arms again. The smaller man shrugged. 'Well, all that may be true, but how do I explain to my wife I'm selling out for a hundred thousand dollars? She's every bit as dedicated as — .'

This time when Dulette interrupted it was loud enough. 'Listen to me; you can tell her that it isn't going to make one bit of difference. Ellingwood was also inno-cent — and what did they do to him? You can tell her that, my friend. They will make Mace or someone like him kill her — and you — and me. You can also say that the longer we hang around here haggling the surer it is that they are going to figure things out.'

'What about Hoffmann?'

'Never mind. I'll handle Hoffmann. He's nobody in any case.'

'And Mace; I suppose he's nobody too.'

'Don't be cute with me. Mace will disappear. Now, now, don't get that look on your face. Leave Mace to me. You don't have to say a thing about him to your wife. If she doesn't know he's in Hamilton, don't tell her. Now get along, do what you must, and get back here as soon as you can. I give you my word, we just don't have all the time in the world.'

'Someone is suspicious?'

'No, of course not. But it takes time to make a good escape. Every second we can use getting out of the country means that we are that much farther away from ever being caught again. Now go, will you, and hurry back. *Go*, damn it!'

Waltham eased the trapdoor down very gently, let his breath out, drew in a fresh breath and tried to imagine why Frank Lee, old Kingsley's son who had inherited so much wealth, was involved in anything as sordid and pointless as this?

There were always greedy people around, but they weren't all so foolish as to get mixed up with someone like Armand Dulette; particularly when they could buy and sell men like Dulette and didn't need that hundred thousand, which they would, in this case, be paying a terrible price to get hold of.

Waltham fell back on that old conviction about people whose ideologies differed, if they were dedicated enough, abandoning everything to serve a cause. He had seen many people, men and women, sacrifice themselves for that. But this wasn't idealism, this was selling out for a hundred thousand dollars, and for someone like Frank Lee to do that was insane.

Waltham's speculations were interrupted by someone — Dulette undoubtedly — stepping on top of the trapdoor, forcing the edges down all around and cutting out the little knife-blade edges of light. Waltham scarcely breathed. But it was far better to have Dulette standing atop the door than lifting it.

Waltham tried to imagine what he'd be

doing up there. Dulette moved a little, shifting his weight, moving a foot, shuffling left, then right. It was the sharp sound of a small lock snapping into place that gave Waltham his clue. Dulette had done something with those valises up there; possibly he'd taken some of the money out of one valise and put it into the second one.

Waltham eased down sufficiently on the ladder so that he could stand straight; his neck ached from being held to one side for so long. Also, he needed a moment to make a decision.

The best time to jump Armand Dulette was now, while that other Apparatus person was not in the secret room. If the other one returned, along with a woman, it could be sticky. But until Dulette got off the trapdoor Waltham couldn't raise it, either, and each moment that passed increased the chance of the other returning.

Waltham climbed back to the top again and cocked his head sideways to listen. Dulette was not moving at all now, but he was still atop the door; there was no light coming round the edges.

Waltham raked his brain for some solution, came up with nothing at all, and eventually Dulette stepped off the trapdoor, moved slowly towards the southerly end of the vault as though expecting his ally to return, and Waltham drew his belt-gun, took a firm hold on the door above, and gave a mighty heave.

The trapdoor flew up and fell back with a roll of loud sound. Dulette whirled, his face contorted. Waltham sprang out and without taking his eyes off Dulette grabbed the pair of valises and flung them down into the tunnel below, then he gestured with the gun.

'Get down there!'

Dulette was stunned or shocked into temporary immobility. 'You . . . ?' he gasped. 'You . . . ?'

Waltham started forward. He did not have any time for this. He called Dulette a name and curtly gestured towards the trapdoor, then, when the older man still seemed unable to comprehend, Waltham reached to give him a push.

Dulette recoiled, and in that split-second Waltham realised that he'd been trapped. Dulette had doubtless been stunned, but not all *that* stunned. He lunged.

Waltham shoved out a leg, pivoted in a flash and barely got free of the hooked hands reaching for his throat. He swung viciously with the heavy little snub-nosed belt-gun, catching Dulette below the neck but higher than the shoulders. In the fleshly part of the man's back. It wasn't a painful blow because it had missed connecting where it had been aimed — the back of the head — but it added to the heavy man's momentum.

Dulette came around slowly, making a grimace. Waltham levelled the revolver and cocked it. 'For the last time — get down in that damned tunnel!'

Dulette finally moved to obey. He might have stalled in the hope of help arriving, but he didn't, and that was pretty obvious too. He meant to be at the bottom when Waltham started down from the top.

The flashlight lying on the table,

evidently the same torch Dulette had used in reaching this secret place, was long and heavy. Waltham picked it up, flicked it on, and when Dulette raised his contorted face Waltham hit him in the eyes with the beam.

'Start moving along the tunnel the moment you touch down,' he said. 'Try being cute and your tunnel will be your grave. I give you my word on that.'

The light made all the difference. Waltham could keep an eye on his prisoner all the way down, and afterwards, with Dulette standing up ahead thirty or forty feet looking back hopefully, Waltham flicked the torch and saw it light up their tunnel for what he estimated had to be no less than a hundred feet. He gestured.

'Turn around, Dulette, and walk along. We'll maintain this interval. If you turn around or make any unnecessary noise on the way back, I'll kill you. You had better believe me.'

Dulette made no move to turn or to commence walking. 'Wait,' he said. 'Listen, in that valise at your feet there is a half million dollars in cash. I will — .'

Waltham called Dulette that name again. 'Walk! Open your mouth one more time and I'll kill you. *Walk!*'

Dulette still hesitated but when the pistol tipped upwards towards his face, he turned and began walking.

Waltham could have made his prisoner carry the valises. The reason he did not was because he did not want Dulette encumbered in any way. He wanted the man moving freely so that he could detect any unusual movement at once.

He hadn't been bluffing about shooting. They both knew it; these were some of the ground-rules for this game they both played. Under reversed conditions it was entirely plausible that by now Waltham would be dead, and if things had been only a little different from how they now stood Dulette would also have been killed. Waltham needed him alive, but it wasn't mandatory and they both realised this too.

Waltham wanted most of all to get far enough along the tunnel so that when the man he thought was Frank Lee returned, saw the trapdoor open, the valises and Dulette gone, and possibly decided to follow, there would be enough distance between them for Waltham to hear the other man before he and his prisoner were heard.

The larger of the pair of valises began to get heavy before they'd gone very far. The smaller one, tucked under Waltham's left arm, was much lighter. In fact, he speculated that it might be quite empty.

They passed beyond where the chilly little draught had that wood-ash scent to it, which Waltham thought meant they were well away from Hampton House again, perhaps were now passing under the greensward. It was a goodly distance; if Frank Lee came along now he'd have to run to even get close and that tunnel was hardly a place for running, even to someone who was familiar with it.

21

Catching the First Fish

The breeze was cold again and by Waltham's estimate, aided now by a bright light, they were two-thirds of the way back when Dulette took a chance and spoke.

'Let me say something, Waltham.'

'Stop and say it.' Peter wanted to put that heavy valise down and rest a bit anyway. 'Don't turn around, just say what's bothering you.'

'If you take me up through the bedroom, which is the way you came down here, there's a hell of a good chance two men will be waiting for us both.'

'Who are they?' Waltham asked, thinking he knew.

'A man named Hoffmann and another one — .'

'Mace? Forget him.'

Dulette's sagging shoulders firmed up

a little as though surprise had caused that. 'You got Mace?'

'Last night. In the haberdashery store across from the hotel. Don't ask me to guess how he happened to be watching but he was.'

For a moment Dulette was silent, then he swore with great feeling and said, 'He *couldn't* have known about the clothes dummy standing atop the trapdoor.'

Waltham guessed Dulette's difficulty. 'He was. I had moved the dummy and had gone down for a look around, then came back up. He was waiting. Dulette, do you know what that means? It means Mace knew about the tunnel, doesn't it? Knew where the store trapdoor was. In other words, Dulette, he was on the verge of finding the money — and you along with it. You ought to thank me for taking him out of the game.'

Dulette was still stuck on the same thing. 'I don't see how he could have known. Waltham, are you lying? Because if you are, when we climb up into my bedroom — .'

'I'm not lying to you. I have no reason

to. By now Mace is no longer in Vermont.'

'How about Hoffmann?'

'That's enough; start walking and shut up.'

'But Hoffmann isn't friendly either. If he'd — .'

'Hoffmann should be locked in the constable's potato cellar, or whatever he uses as a jail, by now. Walk!'

Dulette stepped out again, aided by the light from the flashlight behind him.

When Waltham picked up the valises the larger of the two had that same heaviness to it. He thought that even if that money inside was all in notes of large denomination, a half million dollars was still quite a bit of dead weight.

They came to the first tunnel, eventually, the one leading up into the store. Waltham halted Dulette directly beneath it. 'Here's where we climb out,' he said.

Dulette contradicted him. 'Not so. This trapdoor can't be opened from below, only from above, and only then when the recessed brass rung is pulled out first.'

Waltham put the valises down, listened for someone hurrying along behind them, heard nothing, and put a close look upon Dulette. After hearing all Dulette had to say about emerging across the street in Dulette's bedroom, it seemed wise to start topside here rather than on over at the hotel. He gestured with the pistol.

'Climb up and open the door,' he ordered.

'I just told you,' protested Dulette. 'It can't be opened from below. Only from above.'

Waltham started to repeat his order, to make Dulette prove his statement, then hesitated. They were wasting time. They would waste much more if Dulette had to climb up there, demonstrate his point and climb down again. He gestured. 'Go on, we'll use the bedroom ladder then.'

The danger on ahead could be real, and then again if only Mace and Hoffmann were the sources of peril, the bedroom could be even safer than the store. In either case, Dulette was going to climb up first, his body making a thick shield for Waltham, and that was a reassuring prospect.

They finally came to the end of the

tunnel. Waltham flashed the light up and gestured. As Dulette turned his head as though to speak Waltham touched a finger to his lips — then grinned. They stood a moment looking at one another. Dulette was no fool, he knew exactly what Waltham was doing. But he finally reached, gripped the ladder and started up.

Waltham came behind him, two rungs lower just in case it occurred to Dulette to drop a booted foot into his face. The climbing was awkward with those valises but he persevered.

The moment Dulette was half into the room Waltham called up to him. 'Lie flat right where you are. Make one jump away from the trapdoor and you get it!'

Dulette made the jump anyway. It was his first, and possibly his only, chance to break away. Waltham heard his body strike and aimed. He had the trigger half depressed when a familiar, garrulous voice said, 'Why don't you obey, Dulette?'

Doctor Clancy!

Waltham heaved the valises over into the room, raised his head gingerly, and saw an odd sight. Clancy was sitting in a chair over by the bedroom door facing the open trapdoor with a shotgun in his hands and that old pistol of his stuck pirate-like into the waistband of his trousers. Leaning behind him in the doorway without any gun visible at all, was the turkey-necked old redfaced constable that Waltham had had pointed out to him his first week in the village. The constable was chewing something, ruminating with the slack-jawed rhythm of an old chewer. Later — several months later in fact — Waltham thought he had been chewing tobacco, all but a lost art everywhere except in rural America.

Dulette was still on all fours, not moving at all, his gaze riveted to the twin barrels of that scattergun which was less than fifteen feet from him. At that range, whether Dulette know it or not, Clancy's shotgun would cut him in two and blow parts of both halves through the wall.

Waltham climbed out, brushed his hands together, smiled and said, 'Just keep him covered, Doctor. I've never had a chance to frisk him.'

Dulette had a gun in a shoulder holster. It was the only weapon unless Waltham felt like including a stag-handled clasp-knife which he also flung over onto the bed. Then he gave Dulette a kick and said, 'Get up. You'd disgrace a dog down on all fours.'

The constable, his mournful gaze never leaving Dulette, produced a pair of antiquated iron cuffs connected by a short length of steel chain and still without speaking, or breaking the rhythm of his moving jaws, went over and locked the cuffs on the prisoner.

Doctor Clancy finally stood up, eased down the dogs on the old shotgun and handed the thing to the constable. 'We took Hoffmann in the store right after we also took Clarence. They're locked up. Constable Ward saw to that.'

Waltham smiled at the older man. 'Open that big valise, Doc.'

Clancy eyed the valise then eyed Waltham. 'What for? Is it perhaps booby-trapped?'

Waltham laughed. 'What kind of books

do you read, Doc? No, it's not booby-trapped. At least it better not be or Dulette goes up with the rest of us. I just wanted you to see what a half million dollars looks like.'

Clancy and Constable Ward opened the valise on the bed beside where Armand Dulette sat looking grey and defeated. For once, the constable's jaws ceased moving and his eyes got round. Clancy picked up several of the green bundles almost reverently. Then he replaced them and shook his head at Dulette.

'Almost, Armand, I don't blame you. Just almost.'

Dulette did not respond except to gaze at the money until Clancy closed the lid and snapped it into the locked position.

The constable, chewing again, said, 'Mister Waltham, Doc and I've had a lot of time to thresh things out and I reckon I understand it all now. Most all of it anyway. But just what am I holdin' Armand on? I mean, folks can't just go sashayin' around putting cuffs on other folks without a fair enough reason. It's ag'in the law in Vermont.'

Waltham controlled the smile that tugged at his lips. 'Lock him up and hold him on any charge you like, Constable. I'll telephone for a federal warrant.'

'But you got to have grounds for one of them too, Mister Waltham.'

Peter nodded towards the valise. 'A half million U.S. dollars smuggled into the country illegally will do for starters, Constable. I'm sure we can dig up plenty else.'

'You're plumb certain are you, Mister Waltham? I realise all that Doc told me is sort of illegal an' all, but a body can fetch up in a heap of mighty serious trouble lockin' folks up nowadays.'

'I'm plumb certain,' Waltham retorted, reassuringly.

Constable Ward subsided briefly, but his mournful expression did not depart, and a moment later he said, 'Well now, what about Clarence Johnson, the store-clerk? I've known him all m'life, Mister Waltham. Grew up with him.'

'What did he have to say about the trapdoor and the tunnel?'

Clancy answered dryly. 'You aren't

272

going to believe this, Peter. Armand told Clarence that was the city water-main down there — used for carrying off winter overflow. He believed him. He said he never looked down there but once in nine years.'

It could have been the truth. New Englanders were not notorious for being folk with soaring imaginations. Waltham said he'd get round to talking with Clarence after some more important things had been taken care of. He then jerked his head at Dulette.

'Get up. He's all yours Constable. Just keep him behind bars until I can make a few telephone calls. I'll be round to see you in a couple of hours, more or less.'

Constable Ward nodded, chewed and thoughtfully regarded the valises. 'What of the evidence, Mister Waltham?'

Peter handed both valises to Doctor Clancy. 'Carry them to the jailhouse for him, will you, Doctor? He'll want to lock them up too.'

Clancy accepted the valises but didn't look quite pleased. 'What are you up to now?' he asked.

Waltham pointed downward. 'Back through the tunnel again. He had a friend out there. I want him too.'

Clancy nodded. 'Where does it go — or is that a secret?'

'Out to Hampton House, Doctor, and up into a long, narrow place behind the fireplace.'

Constable Ward stepped over, peered downward, and shook his head. 'You know, if there was another feller down in there, Mister Waltham, comin' this way — armed — you could be runnin' into a heap of bad trouble. I tell you what I figure might be better'n going down into that hole.'

'What?'

'Give me a hand lockin' up Armand, here, and then the two of you can drive out to the manor house on *top* of the ground, whilst I sit in here with the shotgun in case he comes a-scooting along in the tunnel. That way, no matter which way he jumps, we got him. By the way — who *is* he?'

Waltham knew the reaction before he said the name, so he hesitated and saw

Dulette gazing at him. He shrugged. 'Answer the man,' he said to Dulette, and got a sneer.

'I answer no one, and from this minute on I say nothing.'

Waltham shrugged and turned. 'I'm not sure,' he said. Clancy and the constable were looking directly at him as though dissatisfied with that, so he sighed and said, 'Frank Lee — I think.'

Clancy gasped and again the constable's moving jaws grew still. Clancy recovered first. 'That doesn't make any sense at all.' He was indignant. He was also very logical. 'Frank is rich. What the hell difference would five hundred thousand dollars mean to him?'

'Doctor, I can only operate on what I see and know,' Waltham replied, slightly exasperated. 'I saw Dulette talking to someone in that secret room behind the fireplace. The height and build were right.'

Constable Ward had recovered his aplomb and now, acting as though dark intrigue were his daily fare he said, 'Well; let's get Armand locked up — together with all that money — and get set for whatever comes next.'

Not until the four of them walked out into the lobby — and old Tom's jaw dropped straight down at sight of his employer wearing the constable's old handcuffs — did Waltham realise that it was broad daylight. That, in fact, it was past ten o'clock in the morning of a crisp, late summer day.

There was more gawking as they walked out upon the sidewalk, trooping along behind Constable Ward, who was carrying his wicked old double-barrelled shotgun, chewing impassively as he strode along, heading for his village jailhouse.

22

A Matter of Ideals

The constable's plan was feasible so they adopted it. While the constable sat in Dulette's bedroom at the hotel with his shotgun, Waltham and Doctor Clancy drove out to the manor house. As they came within sight of the private entrance Clancy said, 'Well, what do you say to them? Or do you pull a gun to make the arrest?'

Waltham looked around, pained. 'No, Doctor, I don't use a gun to make the arrest. I'm not even going to make an arrest until we've sat and talked for a bit.'

Clancy looked relieved. 'It's been an interesting night,' he murmured, and yawned. 'But I've thought it over, Peter, and come to the conclusion that the practice of medicine is really my cup of tea. Not that the danger doesn't cause exhilaration, mind; it's just that one loses too much rest. Twenty years back, though . . . ' Clancy grinned, then they both laughed. Afterwards the old man made a practical observation. 'They may not even admit us to the house. You, for instance, my boy — you look like a genuine villain in that rumpled clothing and with that dark whisker-shadow.'

They'd had one cup of coffee each at the constable's office. It was a poor substitute for a decent warm meal, but it helped sufficiently for Waltham to smile again as he said, 'I'm not going to court them, Doctor, only perhaps talk a bit, then arrest one of them.' He looked down. 'Unless you want to project a most unorthodox image for a medical man, I'd suggest you either button your coat or leave that horse-pistol in the car.'

Clancy glanced down where the butt of his revolver showed, then buttoned his coat.

They turned in and approached the house with a golden day all around, although the heat was not as strong as it had previously been.

Emily and Frank Lee were out front

and saw the approaching car. Before Waltham got close it occurred to him that this might be an ideal situation, providing he could get Mrs Lee to go inside, or go somewhere in order that he might talk to her husband alone.

'Doctor, can you take the woman inside and leave me alone with Lee?'

Clancy sighed. 'I can try,' he said. 'But it makes me feel like a traitor. Isn't there a better way?'

Waltham shook his head. 'There's never a better way to make an arrest than just to make it.' He eased the car to a halt, responded to the Lees' wave with a smile, and alighted. Emily and her husband walked on over. Doctor Clancy climbed out stiffly and walked round the car looking glum.

Frank looked at the two of them. 'Something wrong?' he asked, evidently struck by their solemn and unkempt appearance.

Emily said, 'If you have troubles, gentlemen, it must be the day for them.'

Waltham took that up at once. 'You are having trouble out here?'

Emily flashed her dark-eyed smile. 'Our hired help quit this morning.'

Waltham turned slowly and exchanged a look with Clancy, then turned back. Carl Bronson and Frank Lee were about the same size. Until this moment, though, it had not crossed Waltham's mind Bronson might be the person he was after.

Emily gestured. 'They didn't give much notice,' she said. 'They quit at breakfast and are loading their car over there right now.'

Clancy said, 'Thank heaven,' and unbuttoned his coat, perhaps unconsciously, but in any case the big old pistol immediately came into view. Emily and her husband stared.

She said, 'Doctor . . . ?'

Waltham was already moving across the yard towards the garage-area. Clancy started to follow but Peter waved him back. 'You fill them in,' he said, meaning for Clancy to explain what was happening to the Lees.

When Waltham entered the opened garage where Carl Bronson was bending over the back of his car, pale and nervous, he waited. Bronson finished placing a large cardboard box beside other boxes, then straightened up and saw Waltham looking at him. Bronson froze in his tracks.

'Leaving?' Waltham asked not unpleasantly.

Bronson nodded, shooting a sidewards look towards the doorway as though expecting someone to appear over there. His wife, probably.

'Sudden, isn't it?' asked Waltham, and Bronson forced a crooked smile.

'We've talked of it for a bit.'

Waltham nodded. 'I'm sure you have. Mister Bronson you are under arrest.'

The pale face froze and the man's eyes seemed to waver. He struggled hard for the courage to act indignant. 'Since when is quitting a job grounds for anything like that, and who are you to say such a thing?'

Waltham stood silently trading stares with the man. Very few people, indeed, gave in to defeat gracefully. 'Dulette is in custody, Mister Bronson. So is the half million dollars. Mace and a man called Hoffmann are also under arrest. The tunnel is no longer a secret. Maybe if you hadn't taken so long to make up your mind to flee with Dulette — after the talk in the vault behind the fireplace — you might have got away; at least you might have got a head start on us.'

Bronson breathed deeply and looked again over towards the garage doorway. 'We've done nothing wrong,' he said, and leaned on the side of his car. 'There's no law that says we have to hold the same political views you do, Mister Waltham.'

Mrs Bronson, her arms full of clothing, walked into the garage starting to speak to her husband, saw him, saw Peter Waltham, and in a flash seemed to grasp that things were not going well. She stared at Waltham and said, 'Good morning.'

He nodded at her but it was Bronson who spoke up. 'He's an officer, Dorothy. He's arresting us.'

She didn't seem as surprised as Waltham expected. Instead of turning pale like her husband, Dorothy Bronson stared directly at Waltham, 'On what grounds?' she demanded.

'Espionage,' said Waltham. 'Drop the clothes please, Mrs Bronson.'

She didn't obey, but Walter Lee appeared behind her in the doorway in time to hear the last words Waltham had spoken. *He* looked surprised; in fact, Walter looked stunned.

Mrs Bronson, hearing Walter, turned her head, saw him behind her, and finally obeyed. The clothing fell in a heap at her feet. She had a holstered automatic pistol of small calibre dangling from an arm, previously hidden by the clothing. Waltham nodded.

'Drop that too, Mrs Bronson.'

He raised his right hand to the height of his coat pocket but otherwise made no move to reach the gun beneath. Walter finally said, 'What in the hell . . . ?'

Mrs Bronson let the holstered weapon drop atop the clothing in front of her, turned, stricken finally, and looked wordlessly at her husband. He appeared close to collapse. Too much agitation over the past few hours had sapped the man, had undermined whatever confidence and courage he might have once had. Now, Waltham thought he was confused.

Walter stepped round Mrs Bronson, saw the holstered weapon at her feet, saw the look on her face, on the faces of her husband and Peter Waltham, and screwed up his face in perplexity.

'Peter . . . ?'

Waltham said, 'Later, Walter.' He then said, 'Mr Bronson, turn around, put your hands atop your car and push your feet back until you are leaning.'

Bronson obeyed, finally completely cowed. Waltham frisked the man, found no weapon, and stepped back as Clancy and Frank Lee, followed by Emily whose large eyes were as round as agates, came over and stopped just beyond the large, opened front door of the garage.

Clancy said, 'By the way, Frank, there *is* a secret room behind the fireplace. If you'd torn *that* wall out instead of the other one, you'd have stumbled on to something right enough.'

The Lees were mostly silent through what ensued, quite understandably; what had appeared as a domestic unpleasantness had turned into something altogether different.

The only one missing was Janet Bothwell and although Waltham kept expecting her to appear behind Walter, over by the door that led from the back of the house, she never did. In fact, although Waltham forgot about it after a bit, when he later made enquiry he was informed that she had returned to Boston earlier that morning; right after breakfast.

Frank Lee stepped closer to his servant and said, 'Bronson? Is this what it was all about when you quit this morning?'

It was the woman who answered, not the man. Dorothy Bronson had whatever strength was left to that duo. 'It was this,' she stated. 'But it was a lot more than you know, Mister Lee.'

Emily's black eyes lingered on the Bronson woman's face. 'Dorothy — why?'

Waltham, watching and listening, thought he detected some rapport between the women. He was sure of it when Dorothy Bronson finally let her shoulders sag, and smiled a little.

'It goes back a long time. To when Carl and I met at a meeting up in Canada.' Mrs Bronson clasped both hands in front of her stomach. 'It seemed very right then, Mrs Lee. Now . . . ' she looked gently at her crestfallen husband. 'Now . . . it doesn't seem very right at all.'

Waltham understood although he was certain none of the Lees did. It was simply the case of people adhering to a revolutionary ideal far too long. As happened with all ideals, this one that the Bronson's had served — Dulette and Mace and all the others had also served — just was no longer valid, and the bitterness that was worse than acid to all those people was the fact that, with youth gone, with the middle years nigh, realisation of failure was something that crushed every spirit. It was too late to start anew.

Waltham said, 'I'm interested in something in particular, Mrs Bronson: Did your husband convince you that the pair of you should take the one hundred thousand dollars and run for it?'

Dorothy Bronson gazed at Waltham

with none of the earlier hostility left. 'We argued,' she said, speaking candidly. 'Of course he was right. He said we should take the money and start over somewhere else; that not only wasn't the world revolution going to come in our lifetimes, but it was probably *never* going to come. He told me we had been very idealistic but not very practical. Yes, Mister Waltham, we were going to take the money.'

Clancy buttoned his coat to conceal the old revolver and as he did so he looked up to say, 'I think you people were at least honest.' His gaze settled upon Waltham. 'Dulette — well — I think he saw the handwriting on the wall before you people did, and defected earlier. But for that I like him the less.' Clancy then smiled. 'But then, I've always been a romanticist, in my own idealistic way.'

Waltham caught Carl Bronson's attention and jerked his head. 'To my car, please.'

Bronson obediently started away. His wife caught up, felt for his hand and gripped it. Frank Lee and Emily, touched, turned to Peter Waltham. He knew what they'd say and gently shook his head.

'I'm only the man who brings them in.'

He and Clancy also went out to the car. Walter caught up but his parents still stood back in the garage opening. Walter laid a hand lightly upon Waltham's arm.

'What are their chances?'

Waltham thought a moment. 'The evidence is good, Walter; there will be statements from the others in custody. I'd say they'll end up in prison. But Armand Dulette's the one who'll really get it in the neck.'

Walter, who had heard nothing until he'd come from the house to the garage, had not known Dulette was implicated until this moment. He looked aghast. 'Dulette? Armand Dulette?'

Waltham started the car and Clancy, sitting sideways on the other side of the passenger's seat, said, 'Come by my house in a day or two. Maybe I can thresh it out for you.' He waved as the car shot ahead, and by the time they'd reached the county road Clancy was beginning to feel more cheerful than he had back there at the house. He looked at the mute couple in the back and shook his head.

'Why is it that when we are young we are so certain that the only solution to everything is violence — is the overthrow of governments?' He didn't allow either of the Bronson's to answer, which they didn't seem much inclined to do anyway, sitting together back there slumped and grey and demoralised.

'I think it is because we are so pathetically ignorant of what living is all about. There has never been a really ideal government anyway. Revolutionaries, if they succeed, can't change anything. Man is simply man; that's about the size of it, don't you think? He can't shake free of what he is and therefore he can't create any perfection *better* than he is.'

Waltham, who had been listening closely, now said, 'But he *will* try, Doctor. Maybe that's the answer. He *will* keep trying.'

Clancy shrugged, saw the village ahead on his left and blew out a big, ragged breath. 'Now what, Peter?'

'It will be out of my hands as soon as these two are locked up, along with Dulette and Hoffman.'

'And then?'

Waltham looked over. He liked old Clancy and he'd miss him. 'Florida, I hope. This time of year it's nice down there, while up here — well — winter'll be coming soon.'

Doctor Clancy said no more as they entered town and headed directly for the old stone police station. In every man's life there is one epoch of true adventure. For most men it occurs in youth but for Horace Clancy it had happened long after youth was just a memory. Still, he'd enjoyed it.

He mumbled something about the town having to allocate some of the tax receipts into a special fund 'to plug up that confounded tunnel!' as the car slid to a halt and Waltham finally dared relax, his latest assignment completed.